As a child, veterinarian Pamela Wilson always used to run away from home to get attention from her status-conscious, preoccupied parents. Years ago she met a man who loved her unreservedly, but her parents didn't approve of his blue-collar job, so she ran away from him too. When the ambitious lawyer she's marrying answers a phone call while she's walking down the aisle, it's the last straw! She runs away again— this time to a cabin her parents don't know about, owned by the mechanic. Does he still own it and is he still single? Will she finally stop running away and make the right choice?

This book was previously published under the title The Reluctant Bride.

The Right Choice
Copyright © 2020 Fiona McGier
ISBN: 978-1-4874-3079-5
Cover art by Martine Jardin

Published by eXtasy Books Inc or
Devine Destinies, an imprint of eXtasy Books Inc

Look for us online at:
www.eXtasybooks.com or www.devinedestinies.com

The Right Choice

By

Fiona McGier

CHAPTER ONE

Pamela twirled around in her gown, letting her mother see the full effect of the swirling skirt, with the veil floating in the air around her head. "Well? What do you think, Mom?"

Maribel sighed. "Honey, even if you weren't my daughter, I'd think you were the most beautiful bride I'd ever seen! And the fact that you are wearing a dress that I designed just makes it that much more of a special thrill for me. You are so gorgeous!"

Maribel moved closer to hug her daughter, and they both smiled as she aimed a gentle kiss at Pamela's cheek, but stopped just short of making contact. That way there was no danger of smearing the makeup which had been so painstakingly applied that morning.

Pamela giggled. "Not like you are prejudiced or anything, right Mom?"

Maribel shook her head firmly. "No. You are breath-taking my dear, and the dress is divine."

Pamela frowned at her mother while she looked into the mirror and met her eye in its reflection. "I still think the dress should have been more of a cream color, though. I mean, it's too — too white. It's not like I haven't been living with my intended for the past two months now. We certainly aren't angels deserving of pure white."

Her mother raised her eyebrows and shook her head. "Don't be ridiculous, Pam, dear. No one is virginal on their wedding day anymore. At least they shouldn't be. Why even back when I married your father, I wanted to *try him out* before we got married. And he felt the same way."

Pamela giggled at her mother's easy admitting of something she had denied to her daughter for years. "That's not what you used to say."

Maribel rolled her eyes. "But that was when you were a teenager, and way too young to be engaging in sexual intercourse with anyone. Now you are an adult, and so is your groom." She moved closer to smooth out a fold, to pat the skirt back into the perfect arrangement that only she could see. "Besides, a cream color would not have been so spectacular with your skin tone. It's perfectly set off by the stark white of the dress. That's the effect I was aiming for. Heavens, girl, I could lie in a tanning booth for twelve-hours-a-day for a week, and still not have the lovely color to my skin that you have. And you have beautiful curls, and those gorgeous soft brown eyes. Donald is such a lucky man."

Pamela made a face at herself in the full-length mirror while she smoothed down imaginary wrinkles in the dress. "I hope he stops texting and taking calls from his office long enough to notice that!"

Maribel raised her eyebrows in surprise.

Pamela shook her head, making her curls bounce. "Mom, you know it's true. I can't ever get him to take his damn bluetooth out of his ear. That phone of his is always taking his attention away from me."

Maribel shook her head. "Now, honey." She switched to her mother-lecture voice. "You know how close he is to making full partner in his firm. He's thirty-five and not getting any younger. But he's been doing so well, that he's almost there. Once that gets offered, you two won't have to ever worry about your finances again."

Pamela turned to regard her mother soberly. "But will I ever be able to get his undivided attention? Ever? Mom, he even keeps the damned thing on the nightstand next to the bed! If it beeps at him while we are making love, he tries to hide it, but he looks at it, to see how urgent it is. For crying out loud, even while he is supposed to be thinking only of me, he's worrying about his damn job."

Maribel shook her head again. "Pamela, that's what it's like being married to a driven, career man. Your father was like that in his younger days. Many's the times he missed dinner — or canceled our dates, because he had to stay in the office to deal with clients. Your father was the first Black lawyer to make full partner in his firm. You'd better believe that if he'd had a portable mini-computer back then, he'd have had it on even while we were in bed. And I would have supported him doing it. It's a cut-throat world out there. You need to grab every advantage that you can, if you want to succeed and get ahead."

Pamela sighed heavily. "I guess so. But I just wish that I could feel like I'm as important to him as his job is."

Maribel lit a cigarette, looking around for an ashtray. When she didn't see one, she pulled a tiny gold box out of her purse and opened it up. There was a small holder for her to rest her cigarette on, while she poured herself another glass of champagne out of the open bottle.

"Pamela, you *are* important to him. Every partner needs to have a wife. You will be expected to help him to entertain his clients, and to go with him to company functions. There's so much to do once he makes full-partner, that he won't be able to keep up with everything without your help. So you will know just *how* important you are to him then. You'll see."

Pamela made another face at her mother, before drinking the rest of her glass of champagne in rapid gulps. She belched in a most unladylike manner, shooting a guilty look at her mother as she poured herself another glass also.

Maribel glared at her. "Was that really necessary?"

Pamela shrugged. "Yes. It's to remind me that I'm still me.

That in spite of this gorgeous dress that you designed for me, and this ridiculously fussy hairdo that you insisted on, and this perfect makeup that I'll never be able to recreate even if I wanted to, that I'm still Pamela Wilson. I'm the bi-racial daughter of Joseph and Maribel Wilson. I got teased unmercifully for the way I looked when I was in all of those expensive schools you sent me to. My only defense was to be myself and act like I didn't care. I'm now a vet who takes care of people's overly pampered dogs and cats. I don't smoke, though I sometimes drink too much, and I've been known to belch and fart in public, when the spirit moves me. My mother has been trying for years to make me over into the kind of lady that she brought me up to be, but I've been resisting her for as long as I can remember. So there!" She defiantly stuck her tongue out at her mother.

Maribel smiled and shook her head. "Honestly, you were a willful child, Pamela, always butting heads with me. I thought you had outgrown your need to rebel against what you see as the constraints of proper behavior. Donald has been so good for you, helping to ease you into society by taking you to the best places, making sure you would be seen everywhere with him. Don't be a fool and risk everything now, by throwing one of your silly tantrums."

Pamela finished the champagne in her glass and reached for the bottle again, only to have her hand slapped quickly by her mother, who took the bottle and emptied the last of it into her own glass. "No! No more for you until the ceremony is over. I don't want you embarrassing yourself by belching in church, or slurring while you are repeating what will be the most important words of your life. I'm going outside now, to make sure that everything is ready. It's almost time for you to walk down the aisle. I'll be back in here as soon as I can, to let you know when you need to come out."

"Yes, Mother." There was an edge to her voice.

The sarcasm was lost on Maribel. She stubbed out her cigarette, put it and the container back into her purse, then turned to go out the door in a swish of expensive perfume.

With a heavy sigh, Pamela defied her mother's orders and sat down on the chair her mother had just vacated, heedless of the wrinkles she was surely causing in the expensive fabric. She checked her watch, hidden inside of the tiny wristlet that she had insisted she be allowed to wear as she walked down the aisle. It also held her cell phone, her debit card, a little bit of cash, her keys, and her driver's license.

She shook her head, speaking aloud as if her groom was in the room. "Almost time. Donald, you'd better have turned off your blue-tooth, like I asked you to. No phone, no glowing blue earbud. Not during the ceremony, the reception, or the wedding night at the hotel. For just this one day, I want to feel like I'm the most important thing you are thinking about. Not your boss, not your clients. *Me.* Your soon-to-be wife." She glared at herself in the mirror. "Or there's gonna be hell to pay, and I'm just the bitch to collect the toll." She defiantly stuck her tongue out at her reflection. She turned her head slightly to stare moodily out the window, which was her version of patiently waiting. She tried to will herself to be happy and calm, wondering why her stomach still had butterflies in it. *Calm down in there.* The fluttering ignored her.

She tipped the empty champagne bottle into her mouth but got only a tiny drop that her mother had left in it. She resumed staring out the window.

Chapter Two

Ten minutes later Maribel bustled in the door, in a buzz of excitement. "You should see just how many people are here! I swear, half of the movers and shakers from the city are out there. I recognized a few lawyers from your dad's firm, along with the owners of Donald's firm. Of course, none of their wives look anywhere near as gorgeous as you, Pamela. But no one is allowed to out-shine the bride."

Pamela had jumped up from the chair when the door was pushed open, and she was glad to see that her mother didn't appear to have noticed that she was sitting down in her designer gown. She nervously smoothed the obvious wrinkles out and tried to peer around her mother, out the door. "Did you see Donald? Did he take his blue-tooth out of his ear? Is his phone turned off? How does he look? As nervous as I feel?"

"Goodness, all of these questions. Let's see — yes — yes — I think so — totally handsome — and probably. There, now are you happy?"

Pamela sighed and smiled, while she nodded at her mother. "Yes. I'm ready to walk down the aisle now. It's time, isn't it?"

"Yes, honey. Your brother is already up at the altar with Donald, and Angela is waiting at the doorway to the church, so that she can walk right in front of you. Are you ready for your big moment?"

Pamela took a deep breath, trying to ignore the butterflies still flitting around, trapped in her stomach. She nodded. "As ready as I'll ever be, I guess. Let's get this show on the road."

Maribel made a face at her. "Try to sound a little classier when you are in the receiving line, okay? Try not to sound like you're talking to your patients."

Pamela sniffed. "But Mom, *they* don't care what I say, as long as my tone is pleasant. It would be so much easier in life if people were the same way."

Maribel nodded in a distracted manner, as she ushered Pamela towards the door. "Yes, yes, dear, I'm sure it would be — if you say so. What on earth did you do to the back of this dress? Where did all of these wrinkles come from? Damn it! If there was time I'd use a blow dryer on you to smooth them out. No time now. The music has started. Come on, honey. Time to shine."

Pamela picked up her flower bouquet as she walked out of the room and headed over to the doorway that led to the main aisle of the church. Her mother was right, the place was packed! She tried to smile at her sister-in-law, who stood patiently waiting for her, so that she could start her trip down the aisle.

Oh no. My lips are so dry they're sticking to my teeth when I try to smile. What if there's lipstick on them too? I should have checked. She licked her lips nervously, but to no avail. She bit her tongue, trying to force some moisture into her mouth, and was so preoccupied that she almost tripped over a bulge in the carpet that was right before the doorway. She jerked herself upright, hitting the side of the doorjamb with her flowers, knocking a few petals off. She flashed an apologetic smile at the people sitting in the back. *I have no idea who they are. I'll probably never see them again. Who cares if they saw me being clumsy?*

She swore she heard her mother hiss at her. "Regal, Pamela. Remember, you are a princess. Walk like one. Glide, honey, glide." As a child, she had always hated when her mother made her practice walking like that, sometimes with a book on her head. She was at least six inches taller, and quite a bit more voluptuous than her diminutive mother, who made gliding look easy. She got her height from her father. He always said he enjoyed going for walks with her partly because her mother would refuse to come with them, to give them time to be alone together. But also, that way they could both enjoy stretching their legs, taking long strides, racing each other to see who could outlast the other.

But Pamela could see her mother up ahead of her, waiting in the first row of seats behind the altar. So she knew she was only hearing a phantom-whisper from her past. She concentrated on putting one foot in front of the other, trying to walk gracefully, as if it was as natural to her as it was to Maribel. And as it apparently was to her tiny, bird-like sister-in-law, who was almost mincing down the aisle, as if her feet were on fire.

Pamela tried to duplicate those tiny steps, but felt her ankle twist, unaccustomed as she was to the height of the heels that her mother had insisted that she wear to show off her legs, visible through the diaphanous panels on each side of the gown. She quickly regained her balance, sweating profusely in her fear of tripping over something on her way down the aisle. Numerous cameras were flashing all around her. Her anxiety led her to imagine how amused everyone would be to get a picture of her falling—and how mortified her mother would be.

To try to regain control over her nerves, Pamela stopped looking at the people who were standing to watch her walk in, and instead looked up ahead, to see how her bridegroom looked in his tux. His eyes met hers, and she saw admiration and love in them. She let out a breath and smiled back at him.

Just a few more feet. She was busy praying that she would be able to make it all the way up to the altar without any untoward incidents. Suddenly Donald's hand went into his jacket pocket, and he looked downward. He glanced quickly up again, looking beseechingly into her eyes, then he turned slightly so that his back was to most of the audience.

But Pamela didn't need to wonder what he was doing. *What the hell! He's checking his fucking phone? I'll kill him when I get up there!*

She heard her mother hiss at her from right next to her. "Leave him be, Pamela. He knows what he has to do."

She gave her mother a look of betrayal. She looked past her to her father, who was watching Donald with a look of amazed disgust on his face.

"Now?" Pamela mouthed at her groom.

He shrugged, nodding in resignation.

Pamela was close enough to speak so that those on the altar would hear her, as well as those in the first aisle, but no one else. So she took advantage of that and spoke out loud. "Turn that damn thing off right now, Donald O'Reilly! I swear, if you don't, I'm walking out on you, and there won't be a wedding."

He didn't seem to have heard her, not even turning to glance in her direction. So Pamela spoke again, slightly louder. "I said turn it off, now!"

He shot her a quick, furious look. "I can't," he hissed at her. "It's a major client. This is very important. I've been waiting to hear from him for days. It'll just be another minute."

"Very important?" Her voice should have warned him just how angry she was, with a shrill note entering into her normally lower-alto tone. "More important than your bride? More important than your wedding? More important than making me feel as if I'm the most important thing in your life? For just this one damn day?"

There was an audible gasp from many of the guests, including her mother, at her use of profanity in a house of God.

"Almost done," he said through gritted teeth, turning slightly away from the audience again. It looked like he was turning his back on her also.

"Fine!" She hissed at him. "Fine. You just finish up. Take your time. I'm thirsty and I need to pee. I'll be right back. Maybe you'll be done by then!"

She turned to the right and walked along the front row over to the door and went through it, into the quiet hall that led to the rest rooms and the kitchen area. She could hear the guests audibly reacting to her strange behavior, but she was so mad at her bridegroom at that moment, that she didn't care if they all started to yell at her. She had to get out of that church immediately, and get something to drink, to calm her nerves. As she turned the corner at the far end of the hallway, she heard the door being thrown open behind her, letting her know that someone was coming after her. That was the final straw.

I don't want to talk to anyone! Especially not mother, with one of her lectures. Not today! Not now! As a teenager, she had always felt that the worst possible punishment was being forced to sit down facing her mother to explain her behavior. Her mother had never felt a need to rebel in her life. She never understood.

Pamela started to trot, then realized that she had to pick up the front of her dress, or risk stepping on it and tripping herself. *That's all I need now: a bloody nose or a black eye, in addition to my wounded pride.* Once the skirt was out of the way, she began to sprint. The door at the end of the hallway beckoned to her, and she flew out of it like the hounds of hell were after her.

She squinted in the sunlight, looking around desperately for an escape. The limo driver was sitting on a bench under a crabapple tree that was in full bloom. His head lolled back, and his eyes were closed, as he slowly inhaled his cigarette, blowing lazy smoke rings up toward the flowers. The limo was right in front of her, and with the front windows open, she could see that the dashboard was all lit up, so the car was turned on. She kicked off her heels and left them by the bushes that bordered the sidewalk. She raced along towards the limo, staying alert to the door behind her, which was still closed.

Just as she got to the driver's side door, she turned her head to look back. The door was thrown open. Her mother spilled out of it, followed closely by her father. Right behind both of them was Donald, his blue-tooth still flashing brightly, as he stopped to catch his breath.

Furiously Pamela yanked the door open and climbed into the driver's seat. She quickly pulled on the seatbelt, put the car into gear and floored it. With a squeal that was really gratifying, all four tires left rubber on the pavement, as she sped out of the driveway and onto the street. She could see people standing in the middle of the driveway behind her, gesticulating, and her phone started to vibrate inside of her wristlet. She ignored it and kept on driving.

After she had put a couple of miles between her and the church, she started to wonder what to do next. *Where do I go now? Where can I go that they won't be able to find me? I'm not going back to that stupid church to face all of those people again. Not after Donald disrespected me that way in front of everyone!* At the next stoplight, she turned her phone off, to stop the incessant vibrating and chiming that signaled the voicemails and texts they were sending to her. *I obviously can't keep driving around in a stolen limo, wearing a wedding dress. Already people are pointing at me and waving, smiling and pulling out their cell phones to take my picture.* "Oh, this is so not good!" She moaned aloud. *I've got to ditch this dress and the car. Then go somewhere to hide.*

Suddenly she remembered that she kept a few changes of clothing in her office. Sometimes her patients got over-excited when they were getting examined, and more than once she'd been forced to continue the rest of her day wearing the evidence. It had happened often enough that she brought some clothes in for insurance, just in case she had to go out in public after a long day on the job. She pulled the limo up behind her office and quickly ran in to change clothes. Once she had on a pair of comfortable jeans and a tee shirt, along with her comfortable old sandals and her scratched old pair of sunglasses, she felt much more in control of the situation. She grabbed the large quilted bag that the clothes had been in, glad that there was also a pair of shorts, a change of underwear, an exercise bra, and another tee shirt in there still. Then she carefully folded the dress and placed it onto the front seat of the limo. *Now what?*

The clattering and shrieking of metal-on-metal reminded her that the el was just a block away, as a train navigated the turn and headed into the station. *That's it! I'll take the el. They won't be able to follow me.* She began to walk, satisfied with her plan. Suddenly she had a thought and stopped. *Wait a minute. There's a GPS unit inside of every phone, isn't there? I'm not going to let them track me down using my damn phone. I hate these things. They're the reason I'm not saying "I do" right now.*

She walked back to the limo and tossed the cell phone onto the dress, next to the limo keys. She clicked the button to lock the doors, to make it harder for anyone to steal anything. She slammed the door and began to walk quickly towards the el station, keeping a sharp lookout for anyone she might recognize. She ran up the stairs, two at a time, and bought a transit pass. She moved quickly onto the platform to wait for the next train headed east, intending to lose herself in the crowds heading downtown for a Friday night in the great city of *Chicah-ga.*

Chapter Three

Pamela had not realized just how fast her heartbeat was racing, until she sat on the seat of the el train and it started to move. Suddenly the enormity of what she had done combined with the tension she had been feeling for weeks, and she felt herself dissolve into tears. A woman who was tending to her toddlers took pity on her, handing her a couple of tissues, so she was able to blow her nose and wipe her eyes.

The two little girls regarded her with somber eyes, before poking at their mother, asking her why that nice lady was crying. The mother shushed them, and got them settled down on either side of her so she could read them a book. They kept glancing over at Pamela, but she tried to keep her sobbing quiet, so as not to disturb them. And once the train really got moving, the noise was so loud that no one was able to hear her.

As she watched the girls snuggling next to their mother, she envied them their youth that allowed for them to be so supremely content, while she felt overwhelmed with her adult-sized stress.

Eventually her sobs ended, as she wondered what to do with herself next. *I have some cash on me, and my debit card. But I'd better take more cash out of the nearest ATM, so I can pay for anything I'll need without having to use my card. Too traceable. They're already tracking me. I don't need to make it easy for them.* She actually grinned. *Runaway Pamela strikes again.*

As a child she ran way from home quite a few times. Her parents were always busy, and she often felt neglected. The first time she was about six and decided to go find her *real* parents — the ones who would always have time to play with her and listen to her stories. Her father found her in the park a block away from their townhouse. She was tired, hungry and frightened, and glad for the chance to ride back home in his strong arms. He hugged her so closely that she had no doubt that he had really been worried about her. But it had only taken a couple of weeks for her parents to fall back into their old, familiar patterns. She repeated the pattern of running away often, each time convincing her even more that it was the only way to get their undivided attention.

Her older brother scolded her profusely, each time she was brought back home in disgrace. After all, wasn't he even older than her? Didn't she think that he felt neglected sometimes too? But after all, their parents were doing everything they could to take care of them, and she had to understand that the world didn't revolve around Pamela. She had to learn to be patient and take their attention when they offered it, and not expect more.

It was during one of her episodes that she had found the pregnant stray dog, which had obviously been abandoned in the park. The mutt was thin, unhealthy-looking, and growled menacingly at Pamela when she tried to approach her. Pamela had offered her pieces of her cheese sticks that she had brought along with her in her *survival kit*. She was eleven then, and that time it was her brother, seventeen, who had found her crouched down under an ornamental statue on a busy street corner, with the female dog's head in her lap. When she refused to get into the car with him unless the dog could come also, he had almost left her on the corner.

Once they got home, her mother refused to let her keep the dog. It was her father who saw how important it was to her to be able to help her fellow-runaway. She had nursed Maggie, her first pet, through her delivery and beyond. And that was when she decided to become a veterinarian.

She sighed deeply. *They're following me now. They'll figure out I took either a cab or the el. Funny, I used to want to be found. Now I really don't. I'm fed up! Thirty years old, and I still have to beg people who claim they love me, to pay some attention to me? Enough is enough! But where do I go?*

A movie was a good choice. She would have to walk through a mall to get to the theatre, but once she was in it, she could relax, knowing that no one could see her in there. Now that she thought about it, she realized that heading down-town was not her best choice. Donald had booked them the honeymoon suite in one of the swanky hotels on Michigan Avenue. There was no way she wanted to be anywhere near where he might expect her to turn up.

She got off at the next stop, and located an ATM inside of the station, to take out a large amount of cash. Then she crossed over to the other side of the platform, and caught the next train heading back west. She took it almost to the end of the line, to Harlem Avenue. Leaving the station, she caught a bus to the HIP, the Harlem-Irving Plaza. She was pleased to see on the marquee that the newest spy movie was playing on one of the screens. She bought a ticket and some popcorn and settled down into her seat. She was soon lost in a fantasy of the perfect man who saved the world as we know it, yet who still found the time to treat his woman right. *Ah, happily-ever-after endings. I wonder if I'll ever get one?*

When the movie let out, it was starting to get dark outside. *So where do I spend the night? I took out a lot of cash. I know, I'll get a room out at one of the hotels by the airport. Even if they could track me out there, it would take them a long time to check all of them.*

She took the bus back to the el station, and rode further west, to the River Road station. She caught a bus there and got off after a couple of stops, in the middle of a row of hotels. Since she had no idea which one to stay in, she flipped a coin before heading over to the Hyatt. *Too funny! I was to have spent my wedding night in the Hyatt hotel downtown, and now I'm enjoying their hospitality, but in a place about thirty miles west of where I thought I'd be.*

No one even batted an eye over her paying cash. She signed herself in as *Shelly Silverstein*, in honor of her favorite poet. When she got into her room, she ordered herself a pizza through room service, and added a bottle of sparkling wine to her order. *To celebrate my escape to freedom. Ironic, right? And I'm going to enjoy eating the whole pizza. I've been starving myself for weeks, trying to lose enough weight to make Mom happy with how I looked in the dress. Now I don't care anymore.*

While she waited for her food, she took a shower, before wrapping herself up in the fluffy robe she found in a baggie on the bed. When dinner arrived, she paid cash for it, then set it onto the table and sat down to eat, flipping the TV on to entertain herself. She had finished the pizza and was half-way through the bottle of wine when the ten o'clock news came on. She was just pushing the buttons to change the channel to something more entertaining, when she was shocked to see her own face looking back at her from the screen. Then her image was reduced to a corner of the screen, and she saw Donald being interviewed. He was standing in front of the church. It was obviously filmed early in the afternoon, because the sun rays were bouncing off of the returned limo that he was leaning against. She turned the sound up.

The interviewer was explaining that the aggrieved man's bride had run away from the church earlier that day, and that her family and friends were frantic with worry over her where-abouts. Then she asked Donald if he had anything to add.

He looked directly into the camera to speak. "Pamela, we know you are out there somewhere. Sweetheart, you *know* how much you mean to me. This is all just a huge misunderstanding. Come on back home to me, and we'll reschedule the wedding. I'm going to be in our hotel room tonight, so you'll know where you can find me. I'll be waiting for you. Call me—or at least call your mother. We can work it out. All is forgiven."

Pamela hit the *mute* button before throwing the remote control onto the bed. She jumped up to flip him off on the screen. She yelled at him. "All is forgiven? *You* are forgiving *me*? For what, you asshole? You answered a message from your job *during* our wedding ceremony! That's how much I mean to you. I'm always second in your mind, after your fucking job. I love what I do for a living, but it's not my reason for living. I thought that's what I was to you."

Pamela shocked herself by bursting into tears. She sat down on the bed and wrapped herself up in the quilt, rocking as she sobbed. *I've been looking my whole life for someone to love me so much that nothing else matters to them. I thought that someone was you. I was so wrong. You lied to me. You said you loved me. But you didn't love me enough to turn off your phone for me, not even just for one day.*

Gradually her sobbing grew quieter, and she hiccupped as she took in deep breaths. She grabbed for the water glass she had poured the wine into, taking a big gulp, to stop the hiccups. She stared morosely at the ads on the TV. *Fine. You love your job so damn much? Marry your job. I'm done with you. I'll stick with my dogs and my cats. They love me and don't ignore me when I talk. They listen to me. And they don't care how I look or how I act.*

She finished off the bottle soon after that. When she finally fell asleep, she tossed and turned fitfully, dreaming that she was a rabbit being chased through the woods by one of her biggest patients, a retriever who *dogged* her all through the night.

Chapter Four

When she woke up, Pamela looked out of the window to see a beautiful sunny day. She took a quick shower, then put on the clothes she had been wearing the day before. She wound her hair into a ponytail, as she always did at work to keep the critters from chewing on her curls. *I think I'll go see what's down there in the breakfast nook.*

She looked around the room to be sure that she hadn't forgotten anything, then tossed the wristlet into the bigger bag that still held her change of clothes. She went out into the hall and closed the door behind her, having left the key on the nightstand. *Do I take the elevator, or do I walk? Yeah, like I get so much exercise? Stairs it is, then.* She walked down the hall, heading in the opposite direction from the elevator, to where the exit sign indicated the stairway was located. She opened the door and was half-way through it when she recognized a voice coming from behind her and felt her heart start to race.

"So where is the room you say she's in?" Donald sounded irritated.

"This way, to the left, sir."

Pamela took a quick peek down the hall then hid behind the almost closed door to the stairs and listened to the two men speaking as they walked quickly down the hall, accompanied by a manager who held a pass key.

"Are you sure it was her?"

"Yeah, I'm sure. I saw the news this morning when you were on, showing her picture. I brought her a pizza and a bottle of sparkling wine."

"Sparkling? Yeah, that's her."

"I asked her if she was celebrating something, and she said, *Freedom*. She didn't seem to want to talk much, so then I left."

"What name did you say she used?"

"Shelly Silverstein. I thought it was kind of odd, since she didn't look Jewish."

Donald's voice dripped sarcasm. "You're kidding, right?"

"That's the room, Mr. O'Reilly. Seven-oh-nine."

Donald pounded loudly on the door. "Pamela? Open up, it's me, Donald." No answer. He pounded loudly again. No answer.

"Allow me," the manager said. She unlocked the door, announcing their arrival in through the door. "Ms. Silverstein? I am the hotel manager. We are coming in to check on you now."

Pamela watched the three of them go through the door, then she flew down the stairs with her heart pounding in her chest. *I don't want to see you! I don't want to talk to you! Just leave me alone!* The words repeated themselves over and over in her brain as she pounded down seven flights of stairs, praying that she was quick enough to beat the elevator back down. She knew they would see the key and know that she had already left. She had to be out of the lobby before they got back downstairs.

When she reached the lobby, she glanced quickly at the elevator and was horrified to see the flashing numbers indicating that it was already on the third floor and coming down quickly. She ran for the nearest escape, which was an escalator going down. *Down, towards the street, right?* She pushed people out of the way to get herself onto the escalator and out of sight, before the elevator door opened.

Once at the bottom of the moving stairway, she looked around for an exit, only to realize that she had entered an exhibit area. There were businesspeople milling around at the various booths, in tailored suits. Some regarded her briefly with mild curiosity.

She smiled vaguely around at them, before addressing a pleasant-looking older man near her. "I must have taken a wrong turn. How do I get out onto River Road?"

He smiled and pointed at the escalator. "Well now, little lady," he spoke in a lazy drawl. "Y'all have to go back up that there escalator, then across the lobby to the exit that leads to the parking garage. That's the only way ah know of to get out of here."

A couple of women standing near the man nodded in agreement.

"Thanks," she said quickly as she headed back to the bottom step. She was halfway up the escalator, behind a group of veiled women chattering in a foreign language that she didn't recognize, when she saw Donald being shown to the escalator by the manager. The desk clerk was waving at the escalator.

Pamela pushed closer behind the women, to try to hide behind their flowing veils and voluminous clothing.

That only worked until Donald was right next to her on the opposite side of the escalator. He had been staring downwards, but suddenly glanced up and saw her trying to shrink down to hide. "Pamela! Get off of that escalator right now. Wait for me up there. We need to talk." He tried to push his way back up to the top by walking against the direction the stairs were moving in but found that there was a crowd of people behind him, obviously heading down to the convention floor. Despite his best efforts, the escalator continued to usher him down to the next floor.

Pamela shook her head at him but said nothing. As soon as she reached the top of the stairway, she looked around wildly for the exit sign. She saw it and took off at a sprint towards the parking garage and freedom.

Out of the corner of her eye she saw her father, spilling his coffee as he jumped up from a chair. "Pamela Elizabeth Wilson! You stop right there, young lady!"

She ignored him and kept on running. She ran out into the parking garage, taking only a moment to get her bearings before racing for the stairs. She ran down the stairs two at a time, then pushed open the door onto the hustle and bustle of Saturday morning traffic near the world's busiest airport. *O'Hare! Of course. I can lose them in there.*

Knowing that Donald and her father would have to get their car out of a parking space, she figured she had enough time to run to the el station, so she kept up a steady trot down the two long blocks to the station. Racing into the station, she pushed her pass card into the turnstile and took the stairs two at a time to get up onto the platform. A train heading west was just closing the doors to head out for the last stop on the line—the airport. Pamela stuck her arm into the nearest closing set of doors, and it reacted by opening to let her in.

She pushed into the train and collapsed onto the nearest empty seat, her heart racing, breathing in short gasps, as she tried to recover from her sudden burst of early morning exercise on an empty stomach. Her heart was pounding, her head hurt, and she felt like she was going to throw up. But she had to calm down enough to come up with a plan. *What now? Where can I go to hide?*

She glanced around at her fellow travelers and saw that she was being ignored. *No one recognizes me. Good.* As her breathing slowed down, a plan began to form in her mind. She needed to get away, and she needed to somehow throw Donald and her father off of her track. Years of running away had taught her to think one-step ahead of her pursuers. She used all of her experience to figure out how to proceed.

It was a short ride to the airport where she got off, walking quickly, but not running—she didn't want to draw anyone's attention. Walking over to the shortest ticket line for the nearest airline, she pulled a scrap of paper out of her bag, along with a stub of a pencil. As she waited, she wrote on the paper. When it was her turn at the counter, she smiled at the clerk and handed her the paper.

I am deaf. Can you direct me to the nearest car rental agency?

The reservations clerk smiled at her and nodded. "Can you lip-read?"

Pamela smiled back, nodding, making her thumb and first finger into the sign for a little bit.

The clerk smiled again. "I will give you this map, okay honey? Just follow the arrows I'm drawing on it now, and it shouldn't take you more than a couple of minutes to get to where you can get a car." The clerk handed her the folded map.

She mouthed, "Thank-you," as she turned and strode rapidly in the direction indicated. *That should look to any camera watching us, like I was buying a plane ticket. Now I hope I can rent a car with cash.*

Pamela glanced around often as she walked, but she didn't see any signs of Donald or her father, or that anyone recognized her. When she got to the rental booth she flirted outrageously with the agent, to get him to agree to let her pay cash for the car. She did have to let him scan her license but hoped that it would take a while for anyone to trace her there. Once she was in the car, she drove out of the airport and onto the Kennedy expressway, heading east into the city.

After driving for about twenty minutes, she stopped at a *Dunkin Donuts* to use the bathroom, and to get some breakfast. While in the rest room, she stuck out her tongue at her reflection in the mirror. *God! I look awful! It's a wonder the car agent thought I was worth flirting with. Maybe he's just that desperate. Or that married.* She washed her hands, then splashed cold water onto her face. She ran her wet hands through her hair, to try to flatten some of the curls that were frizzing around her face from a combination of the humidity and her recent exertions.

She took her large coffee, cinnamon roll, and milk carton into her car. She rolled down the windows for a breeze, as she figured out what to do next. Ravenously, she tore into the greasy pastry, and swallowed it with a minimum of chewing to slow her down. She gulped the milk down in a couple of large gulps, then loudly belched out all of the air she had swallowed along with her empty carbs. She smiled at herself in the rear-view mirror. "Take that, Mother. That was a good one, wasn't it?"

She leaned back on the seat and took a tiny swallow of the hot coffee. The enormity of what she had done crashed down on her. *So what do I do now? Where do I go? I can't go home, since then I'll have to talk to them. I'm not ready to do that yet.*

She imagined her parents tag-teaming up on her, joined by Donald.

"Just what were you thinking?"

"What is the meaning of all of this ridiculous running away?"

"Explain yourself, young lady!"

"What are we supposed to tell everyone?"

She sighed. *I don't know what we're going to tell anyone. I don't even know why I ran, except that I've just had enough of not feeling important to anyone who tells me they love me. Either they're all lying, or I'm just not worth loving that much.* A tear squeezed itself out of her eye, and she impatiently brushed it away. *No! I'm not going to cry. I'm going to think of where I can go to hide for a day or two, while I figure out how to extricate myself from the mess I've made of my life.* Another tear trickled out, then another. She sniffed audibly.

She began talking to herself out loud, trying to distract herself from crying. She had developed the habit from working with patients who couldn't tell her what was wrong with them. The sound of her voice calmed them down and helped her to focus. She needed to focus now. "I need a place that my parents and Donald can't find. Somewhere that they don't know about, so I can relax, without having to worry about being found." She closed her eyes to think. Suddenly she got an image in her head of a beach house, secluded in a private area known only to local residents.

Determinedly she started the car and drove out of the parking lot and back onto the highway. *What if he's not there? Maybe one of his relatives will be there. What will I tell them? I don't even have a phone number for him anymore. What if he's there with another woman? With a wife and kids? What if they don't own it anymore?* She shook her head to settle her nerves, speaking sternly to herself. "I'll deal with that when I get there. Maybe I can find some motel around there to stay in for a couple of days, until I get my act together."

Then she was struck with the only real impediment to her plan. Her heart started to beat quickly in her panic. *What if I can't find it? It's been years since he drove me out there—and I didn't do the driving. I watched out the window. What if things will look different now? Then what?* She shook her head again, berating herself for her fears. *What am I? Some kind of helpless female who needs rescuing? If I can't find it, I'll just switch to plan B and find a motel. But I'll be out of the state and far enough away that hopefully no one will recognize me, and I'll be able to chill for a while.*

So she kept on driving. She was arguing with herself in her mind the whole way, not willing to admit, even to herself, her *real* reason for heading out to that particular cabin on the beach in Michigan.

CHAPTER FIVE

Eric Taylor sighed as he closed the hood of the late model BMW he had been working on. He was feeling brain-drained, from trying to figure out what was wrong with it. He was also physically tired from standing on his feet on the concrete floor of the bay for the past six hours. All he really wanted to do was jump on his Harley and head home. Once there, he planned on making himself a couple of burgers, then drinking the better part of a twelve-pack, to try to forget the grueling work week he had just endured.

He strode into the station manager's office and smiled at the old man who was, as always, watching the news station. He hadn't had to read the paper for years, since his boss kept him up on all of the latest news stories.

Marco Robelli smiled at his favorite employee as Eric entered the office to punch out for the day. "Got any big plans for tonight, Eric?"

His tone was jovial. This was the same discussion they had every Saturday afternoon, no matter what time Eric left for the day. He treated Eric like one of his sons, so Eric long ago realized it didn't do any good to get upset over being treated like a kid. Since his own dad was long gone, he just tried to be happy that someone cared about him enough to ask.

Now he just shook his head. "Nah, but there's a twelve-pack waiting for me, and she's been keeping herself cold for me all day long."

Marco nodded, smiling wistfully. "Ah, youth—it's wasted on the young. Why when I was your age, young man, I couldn't wait for Saturday nights, so I could go out dancing. Lots of girls would fall all over themselves, just to find a guy who knew how to dance."

Eric smiled at his boss. "Yeah, but did you ever get them to do the *horizontal bop* with you?"

Marco let out a whoop of laughter. "Sometimes, my boy, sometimes." He looked furtively around the office. "Just don't let on to Mrs. Robelli. She likes to think she was my first."

They both laughed at that.

Marco pointed at the TV screen that he had been keeping one eye on. "Will you look at that? Women today. Who knows what the hell they're thinking?"

Eric had just stepped behind Marco to punch out his time-card, so he had a view of the set that Marco was jabbing his finger at, trying to make a point. "She has a guy like *that* who wants to marry her, and she runs away, leaving him at the altar."

Eric glanced at the set to see a man standing in front of a limo parked in front of a church, talking to a reporter. "He looks like a lawyer—or a trader. In fact, he looks like any one of our customers. I don't know about you, but they are such a pain in the ass to work for, I'd never want to be married to any of those douchebags."

"Yeah, but they always pay their bills on time. And they always buy expensive cars that need extensive work when they break down. Keeps us in business. Now look, there's a picture of her. She's quite a looker. No wonder he's trying so hard to get her back!"

Eric looked up from setting his timecard into the box and stopped breathing. He felt his heart start to pound. He leaned forward to look even closer at the screen.

The talking head doing the interview had stopped speaking, and the man had turned directly into the camera and was talking. The headline scrolling at the bottom of the screen announced, *Plea for runaway bride to come home.*

Marco looked up in surprise at the unaccustomed sight of Eric actually paying attention to the TV that he watched all of the time. "What? You want a better view of the babe in the corner? The gal who ran out on that guy?"

Eric cleared his throat and nodded. "I think I know that girl. I—uh—went to high school with her."

"Ah," Marco nodded wisely. "Ex-girlfriend?"

Eric nodded in a distracted manner. "Yeah, something like that."

Marco gave him a quizzical look, as he slapped his hand on his thigh. "*That's* why she looks so familiar. Isn't she the one who came to see you a coupla years ago? She talked to you back in the shop, then she left in a hurry?"

Eric nodded slowly. "Yeah, that's her."

"Well, she's a looker all right. Any man would be a fool to let her get away."

Eric made a face. "But she's got a really bad habit of always running away. Like she just did. I wonder where she is now?"

Marco shrugged. "Who knows? News says she's been gone over twenty-four hours. I saw this same footage yesterday. Where-ever she is, she must have found a really good place to hide."

Eric's mind raced. "Yeah. Somewhere that no one in her family would know to look for her."

Marco nodded. "Probably."

Eric took a deep breath and turned, walking quickly toward the door.

"Well, it's late. I'm outta here. See you on Monday afternoon, maybe."

Marco laughed. "That beemer isn't going to fix itself, you know. You'd better be here. I'm counting on you."

Eric grinned at his boss. "Yeah, that's what you pay me the big bucks for, I know. See ya."

He strode out of the door and out to his bike, parked in-between his boss' BMW and the shop. He pulled his helmet on and fired up the Harley, letting the throaty roar temporarily deafen anyone in the immediate vicinity.

As he drove out into Saturday afternoon traffic, he tried to clear his head, but his thoughts were racing with a mind of their own. *Nah, there's no way — is there?*

When Eric got back to his apartment, he told himself he was just following his usual routine of checking for messages. That's why he headed towards the phone as soon as he was in the door. The light wasn't blinking, so he went to the fridge and grabbed a beer. He twisted the cap off before taking a large swig. Then he walked back to the phone and sat heavily in the chair next to it. He took another drink from his bottle, then picked up the phone and quickly dialed a number.

His brother picked up the phone on the second ring. "Hello?"

"Hey Jerry, it's me."

"Eric? It's been a while. What's up?"

"I was just wondering — you're not planning on heading out to the cabin this weekend, are you?"

"Nah, got too much going on with the family. Annie's in a local theater production, and Joey is working and needs the car. Maggie gets pissed if I head out there alone, so I'm stuck in town. I gotta work on the yard, so it's probably for the best. Too bad, though. The weather report says it's gonna be gorgeous out there for the next coupla days. Why?"

"Is anyone else there, that you know of? Any of the cousins?"

"No, I don't think so. It's free and clear for you, buddy. Why? Got a new woman to entertain?"

Eric smiled as he shook his head. "A new one? No. But I was thinking of heading out there tonight. Just wanted to be sure I won't be running into anyone."

"It's all yours, dude. Just don't do anything I wouldn't do."

Eric smiled again. "Is there any of my beer left out there??

His brother sounded wounded. "What do you take me for? A mooch? I replaced what I drank, like always. We also left some burger buns there last weekend. Not on purpose, we just forgot about them until we got home. And Maggie left a coupla bottles of chardonnay too. Don't drink it without buying any more. You know what she's like when she's stressed. The sooner I can get an open bottle and a glass in front of her, the better."

"Okay. Just wanted to be sure I can have the place. I'm going to shower and head out there."

"Enjoy, bro. And have one for me, okay?"

Eric grinned into the phone. "Uh, yeah. I will. See ya."

He hung up the phone and finished the last of the beer in his bottle. He looked around without seeing anything, as he gazed meditatively toward the window. *Are you there, or not? I won't know till I get out there. If you're not, then at least I get a weekend on the beach. But if you are?* He tried to ignore the sudden rush of blood flow downward, making his jeans suddenly too tight.

Shower first, change, then I'm hitting the road. He purposefully got up and set his game plan in motion. An hour later, he was taking the exit that would get him onto the expressway that headed out of the city, and under the lake. As he rode, he tried to concentrate on the feel of the wind on his face, and the sheer physical pleasure of riding his Harley into the warm late spring night. And he tried very hard *not* to think about what happened between them the last time he saw her.

Chapter Six

Driving along the highway, Pamela tried not to think about what kind of reception she would get if the owner of the cabin were there. Her mind was flooded with memories from the last two times she had seen Eric.

Four years ago she was upset with him about the ultimatum he tried to insist on. He wanted her to tell her parents that she was still seeing him. She told him for years that since they were paying for her college costs, she wasn't about to tell them anything that would upset them, and possibly cause them to cut off her money supply. She had not openly dated him, or anyone else, for the eight years that she was in college studying to become a veterinarian.

Once she graduated, Eric expected her to tell them about their continuing relationship. He seemed surprised and more upset than she had guessed he would be, when she told him that she still needed her parents' help co-signing for the loan that she needed to start up her veterinary practice. He accused her of being ashamed of him, and of having no intention of ever allowing their relationship to flourish in the light of the day. He basically threw her out of his apartment, telling her that since she felt that way, they were both now free to date other people.

She retorted that they had always been free to do that—*so there!* Then she jumped into her car and drove herself back to her apartment, fuming the whole way. Her anger only lasted as long as it took for her to miss Eric. Once she realized that she wasn't able to jump into her car and go to see him whenever she wanted to, she was struck by a sense of loss deeper than she had ever expected to experience. But she was not ready to cut the purse strings with her parents just yet. She was working hard to establish her practice, but she sometimes needed their help with advertising and promotions.

She tried to convince herself that Eric was being unreasonable. After all, this was her parents he wanted her to upset. But late at night, when she lay in her bed and her body ached with missing him, she found it hard to keep believing that she was the injured party here—that *he* was the one making *her* feel pain. She grudgingly granted that he just might be right, that she really *should* tell her parents they were still seeing each other. But that filled her with fear of their response. She also felt guilty that she didn't feel strong enough to withstand their disapproval. Combined with the pain of missing Eric, her feelings coalesced into a major episode of depression.

She had not told her parents the reason for her grief, but she had no time to wallow in it anyway. Her mother had already begun the serious business of introducing her newly graduated daughter to any eligible young bachelors in her social circle. After a few months of pretending to be what her mother wanted her to be, she met Donald. Now here she was, running away from her fiancé, and back to the man who told her they were better off apart, since they had so little in common. Pamela sighed heavily. *Was he right?*

It had been unexpectedly painful for her to not be able to go to see him whenever the stress in her life got too intense. She was used to both seeking comfort from him and celebrating with him when things went well for her. But she had been hurt by his rejection of her and determined not to give him the satisfaction of having her crawl back to him. Normally she rejected the men that her mother tried to set her up with. But she gritted her teeth and dated a few of them, trying to fit into the lifestyle that her mother seemed to feel was her due. And she tried to forget about the man she had relied on for so many years. After all, since they had nothing in common, and her parents hated him, then there was no point to trying to continue something that should have ended with their high school graduation.

Almost two years later, she had gotten the invitation to the ten-year high school reunion. She almost discarded it without opening it. But then she thought of him and reconsidered. She hadn't seen him in a while, and she wondered what was going on in his life. Was he still riding his Harley around, looking so good that females of all ages would drool when he drove by? Was he still working at the local gas station fixing cars? Had he ever changed his mind, and settled down with anyone? And most importantly, did he ever think about *her* anymore?

She decided that he needed to see how *over him* she was, so she resolutely checked *Yes, attending, no guest,* and had mailed the invitation back quickly, so she wouldn't have time to change her mind. She never even considered asking the man she had just started dating if he was interested in going. Not only would Donald be bored, since he wouldn't know anyone except her, but having him there would not allow for her to spend any time with the guy who was the main reason she wanted to go to the reunion at all. She didn't want to admit, even to herself, that she was still unable to forget him.

She called one of her best friends from high school, who still lived on the west side, near where she had grown up. She called her to touch base on plans for the reunion, knowing that whatever was being planned, Diane would know about it. They made plans for the weekend, then Pamela put it out of her mind as much as she could, until the day she actually drove into the area. She checked into the motel she had booked a room in, telling herself she wouldn't want to drive home after doing any drinking at the reunion.

Once settled in her room, Pamela called her old friend Diane, to be sure that their manicure and pedicure appointment was still on for three, just over an hour away, and to get directions for how to get there. Diane told her, then started in on how irritated she was that her husband's car was still not done, so they would have to take the minivan to the reunion.

"Honestly, you'd think we live in Outer Mongolia or something! For crying out loud, how hard is it to work on BMW's anyway? It's not like no one else has them. But since that asshole Eric seems to be the only one around who knows how to work on them, we are completely at his mercy. We have to wait until he's good and ready to get around to getting our car done. What a pain in the ass! Now we have to drive on a date in the fucking mommy-van. How romantic, right?"

Pamela had stopped breathing when she heard his name. Since Diane was on a rant, she hadn't noticed. Carefully choosing her words, and trying for a neutral tone, Pamela asked, "Eric? Is that the same guy that I dated in senior year? That Eric?"

"Yes, that's him. He's a mechanic down at Marco's place, and he's apparently the only one who can work on foreign cars. It's like he's some kind of weird *car-whisperer*, you know, like that movie where Robert Redford could talk to horses. Say, you're not thinking about him anymore, are you?"

Innocently, Pamela said, "Who? Robert Redford? Nah. He's much too old for me."

Diane made clucking noises into the phone. "Remember who-the-hell you're talking to, girl. I didn't get the reputation I have, for being the *Gossip-Queen,* by not reading between the lines when people talk to me. You're not planning on trying to hook up with him again, are you? Because he's even more trouble than when he was younger. His dad may be gone, but he's drinking enough for both of them. And in the last couple of years, he's gotten himself an ex-wife who's a real piece of work and had a kid with her. He's got a reputation for sleeping around with anything on two legs, once he's had enough to drink. I believe *man-whore* is the term kids use these days. He's been known to be late to work, because he's sleeping off last night's drunk, or nursing his bruises from last night's bar fight, when he tried to pick up someone else's woman. You stay away from him, you hear me?"

Meekly, Pamela agreed. "Yes mother."

"Besides," Diane continued, "I don't think he's going to the dinner anyway. His name wasn't on the list, so he didn't pay. And no matter how much I need him to fix Ted's beemer, I am *so* not letting him in for free. Not when the dinner is costing so much a plate. Did I tell you we're having prime rib?"

"Yes, you did." Pamela tried to stave off the next round of chatter. "I have to go now, so I have time to maybe lie down for a while—maybe take a nap. I have a bit of a headache that I need to get rid of before I meet you at the nails place. Okay?"

There was a pause, with Diane considering the *message-under-the-message* while Pamela held her breath.

Finally, Diane said, "Okay, just be sure to be there on time. They are booked solid now, because of the reunion. My oldest stepchild, Caitlin, the one who is dating already—at fifteen. They grow up so fast these days. Not like when we were young, huh? Anyway, she called yesterday to try to get an appointment, and the earliest they could get her in was Monday. They are booked solid for the weekend. So whatever you are going to do, just be on time, okay?"

"Okay. Three pm sharp. I'll even try to be a few minutes early. Thanks for setting this up for us. See you then. Bye."

She grabbed the local phone book from the nightstand. With trembling hands, she looked up Marco's and found that there was indeed only one place nearby that advertised being able to repair foreign cars. Judging by the address, it was close to the motel—in fact, on the way to the nails place. So after going into the bathroom to nervously check on her makeup and clothes, and stick her tongue out at her own reflection, she grabbed her purse and got back into her car. She intended to poke at her own past, to see what would happen.

Marco's Service Station was easy to find. It was also a gas station, so Pamela decided to use that as her excuse for stopping by. *Just got into the area, needed some gas — yeah, that's it. "Why Eric, what a surprise! I had no idea that you were working here."* She snorted at herself. *Yeah, right. Then what? "Hey baby, let's see if we can still make each other scream all night?" Or maybe I'll say, "I hear you like to hook up. Let's try it doggie-style, because that's always been your favorite."*

She sighed at her own discomfort as she pulled into the station and got out. As she walked up to the mini-store to buy a bottle of water, she peeked into the service bay area. There were two guys working in there, but neither one had long black hair. One had grey hair, and —

"Can I help you find anything, ma'am?" The gum-chewing teenager at the register barely broke through her shock.

Totally numb from having realized that Eric was the other man, the one with the short, spiky black hair with blond streaks in it, Pamela had to force herself to focus enough to buy a bottle of water. She paid for it, then started to wander towards the service bay area.

"Hey, you can't go back there! Read the sign, lady!" The girl pointed to a prominent sign on the door that prohibited customers from entering the service area. As she stood there in confusion, both men looked up from the car, and she found that she started blushing and couldn't stop, as her eyes met Eric's and his eyebrows rose. Feeling like she wanted the floor to open and swallow her, she stood still in confusion, unable to move. The older man with grey hair looked at her, then at Eric, before moving over to the door.

"It's okay, Tina." he said to the girl whose loud voice had

disturbed them all. "I think E.T. knows who she is. I was just going out for a smoke. Want to join me?"

As he walked past Pamela, he winked conspiratorially at her. He held the door open for the girl, who didn't even look old enough to be smoking, to precede him outside.

Realizing that her time was limited, Pamela took a deep breath, and walked past the open door of a tiny office through which she got a glimpse of a white-haired old man sitting staring at a TV screen, and through the prohibited door, to talk to the man she had driven years back in time to see.

"Hi Eric," she said, hoping that her voice sounded more assured out of her head, than it did from inside her head.

"What are you doing back in this neck of the woods?" He busied himself in the engine of the car he was working on.

"I'm here for the reunion."

"Why? I thought you hated everyone you went to school with and weren't ever coming back."

Pamela wished that he would look up, so she could talk to his face, not the top of his head.

"I thought it would be fun to see people. You know — to catch up on what everyone has been doing for the last ten years."

Eric didn't say anything but continued working on the engine.

She addressed the top of his head. "Are you going? It's for both of our schools you know."

"Why would I?" He finally looked up. His eyes were cloudy with anger, as he continued speaking in sharp, clipped tones. "I still live around here. Anyone that we graduated with that I want to talk to is right here. And that means no one. So why would I spend money to hang out with people I don't want to talk to?"

Pamela was having trouble thinking, because her heart was pounding so fast. Her nerves were thrumming, and she knew her hands were shaking. She nervously jammed them into her pockets and continued to talk. "Well, I was hoping that we might get a chance to talk."

Eric lifted an eyebrow. "Judging by your clothes and your Cadillac SUV, I'd say you've been doing pretty good for yourself. Taking care of rich women's purse-puppies must pay well. So you just run along and have fun at the reunion, telling everyone about what a good choice it was for you to get away from here. Enjoy."

He bent back down over the car engine and appeared to study something deep in the back.

"But I was hoping to have a chance to talk with *you*, Eric." She tried unsuccessfully to keep desperation out of her voice.

He straightened back up and looked directly down at her. She lost herself in his piercing blue eyes, now almost gray with emotion. His face had lost its boyish look, and there were tiny wrinkles around his eyes. His stubble was even more pronounced than it had been years ago. Pamela felt weak in the knees, remembering how it had felt on her upper thighs.

"The fact that you are here means that you have already talked to Mrs. Diane Krieger-Wozniak. And you can tell her *hind-ass* that I'm taking time off of working on *her car*, in order to talk to you. I assume she's already told you all about my sordid life over the past few years. It's all true, whatever she says. Case closed. Nothing more to say. See you around."

He bent back into the car hood, once again forcing her to talk to the top of his head.

Pamela was unable to give up without one more try. "I— uh—was hoping that I could have a drink with you. Maybe even a dance, for old times' sake."

He snorted. "You know I don't dance."

She smiled at his hair, speaking without thinking. "Anyone who can do the horizontal bop the way *you* can, can dance!"

He looked up again. Anger flashed in his eyes. "What the

hell do you want from me? You left me, remember? Repeatedly. And it's been years since you even contacted me. I figured you thought about it and realized that I was right. So there's nothing more to talk about. Now if you don't mind, I have work to do."

He turned to get a tool from the shelf behind him.

Pamela grabbed what little pride she had left, hurrying out through the door, and out of the station. She almost ran into the returning mechanic and the teenager, who must have had at least a couple of cigarettes in the time it took for Eric to stomp on her heart. She got into her car, and drove out into traffic, driving all the way back to her motel. She parked in the back lot and dissolved into tears.

Trying to keep an eye on the time, Pamela went back into her room and splashed her face with cold water, then touched up her makeup. Then she sat on the toilet seat and stared numbly at her own reflection. *What did I expect him to do? Thank me for coming back to see him, and offer to make me scream, for old times' sake? What a naïve idiot I've been! This was a huge mistake, and the sooner I get the hell out of here, the better. I'll have to grin and bear it during dinner, then I'll duck out of the dance early and just drive home. There's nothing for me here, anymore.*

When she got to the nails salon, she was five minutes late. Diane peered closely at her and let her get settled into the next chair to soak her feet, before asking her what had happened.

"Nothing. I just fell asleep and didn't get up in time." Pamela avoided looking her in the eye.

"Liar! You went to see *him*, didn't you? After what I told you?" Diane was making clucking noises, like a mother hen.

"He was working on your car, for what it's worth," Pamela said ruefully, while the manicurists worked on their toenails.

She wondered briefly if every single nails place in the country was staffed by tiny Asian women who pretended their English was not good enough to know what their customers gossiped about while their nails were being done. She hoped they wouldn't understand, since she was so embarrassed.

Diane rolled her eyes. "And was it done? I think not. That lazy asshole needs to do a lot less drinking and partying, and a whole lot more working on my car. It's been in there for two days already."

"Could we just not talk about him anymore?" Pamela sighed.

"Aw, honey, what did you expect? That he'd be glad to see you? It's been a long time, you know. I forgive you for not calling *me*, but then, you didn't break *my* heart when you left!"

"Thanks. I feel all better now."

"Hey, I'm just trying to make you see that he's not good for you. He never was." She patted Pamela's hand and continued briskly. "It's long past time for you to move on. Find someone who's a better fit for your life."

"Yeah, that's what my Mom keeps trying to set me up with." She looked around, trying to think of a way to change the subject. "How did he get so good at doing beemers? There weren't any around when we were in high school." Pamela was hoping to distract herself, trying to fight her urge to sob uncontrollably again.

"When his Dad died a couple of years ago, he must have inherited some money. Who knew that old drunk had any to leave him? He went to some trade school up in Kenosha. He was already a pretty good mechanic by then, since he'd been doing it since high school. He took some classes and earned himself some kind of degree thingie that's hanging on the wall in the shop. I guess it taught him how to work on all kinds of foreign cars, because there's a couple of other beemers around—also a couple of Jags. I think the local alderman has a Porsche, and who knows what else there is? The point is that he's the only one who knows how to work on them, so either we pay whatever he charges, or we have to drive for hours to find someone else who can do it. And then it won't be cheaper, and it will take twice as long. So he's got us all over a barrel. I'll bet he really enjoys that."

Pamela sighed again.

Diane reached her hand over and patted her arm in sympathy.

"He's bad news, girl. He got a waitress pregnant a coupla years ago. She was barely old enough to be legal. They got married before the kid was born, then they got divorced before the kid was a year old. He hangs out in the bars until they close, then goes home with whoever'll have him. You can do *way* better than him. You deserve so much more. Forget about that asshole, and let's have some fun tonight."

Not wanting to keep talking about her self-inflicted pain, Pamela smiled bravely at Diane and agreed to do her best to have fun. Both were now moved over to the manicure stations, and Diane launched into gossip galore, about the other girls from their school, and the guys they knew from their brother school. She knew what everyone was up to, whether they had moved out of the area or stayed. She said that was why she had become the class secretary way back when, so that when people wanted information from their graduating class, they had to get it through her. The ten-year reunion had provided a gold mine of information, and Diane was clearly enjoying being *in the know* about everyone who was attending, as well as those who were not.

Pamela took comfort in the fact that Diane really didn't care if she listened too closely or not, so she sat back and let the idle chatter of her old friend wash over her, as she brooded about the man she had spent years running away from, only to run back to him, over and over again.

He's always taken me back before. Why not now? And why do I care so much? Maybe Mom and Diane are right. Maybe it's time to finally forget all about him and find someone more suitable to be involved with.

"So now what?" Pamela was talking out loud to herself again, partly angry at herself for the situation she found herself in, and partly to keep herself from panic, as she tried to remember what exit to take to get to the cabin she had last been to many years ago.

"He didn't want to see me then. What if he's forgotten all about me? What if he still doesn't want to see me?" She swallowed hard. "What if he's married again?" She shook her head resolutely. "I got myself into this. I'm going to get myself out of it also. I just need some time to chill out and think about how."

She forced herself to pay increased attention to the road, because the exit she figured she'd be looking for must be one of the next few she'd pass. When she drove by one that looked familiar, she got off at the exit after that one, then got right back on the highway and headed back to get off on the exit she had missed. She wasn't sure which direction to turn once she got off, so she sat for a moment on the side of the road and considered. She tried to remember which way they had turned and found herself remembering how excited she had been the first time they had gone there, when he had told her they were going to a place his mother owned. Her father, a Chicago cop, had bought it when cabins in Michigan were dirt-cheap, and he had left it to her, his only child. Eric had wheedled the key out of his Dad for the weekend, and they were going to be able to truly relax and enjoy each other there. It was only the second time they had the chance to be in a real bed. After that, they had gone there whenever he was able to get the key.

Pamela pounded on the steering wheel, trying to clear her tired brain. "We got off from the opposite direction that I just did. Then we turned—left or right? Left or right? Did we go under the highway, or not?" She looked around carefully. "Not!" She put the car back into gear and drove in the direction she had chosen. She kept passing by the roads she needed to turn off on but seemed to remember once she had passed them. She turned around a few more times. Eventually she found herself driving along a small back-road that had warning signs on it.

Trespassers will be prosecuted.

Private: residents only.

Eventually she saw landmarks that she remembered, and a few minutes later, triumphantly, she turned from the dirt road into a gravel driveway that hadn't really changed all that much in the ensuing years. She got out of the car and stretched her cramped back muscles in relief.

She walked slowly up to the front door and knocked. *Hmm. All of the windows are closed. There's no lights on. Looks like no one's home.* Despite the obvious lack of response, she knocked repeatedly. Once she gave up, she glanced around in dismay at the desolate area she was in. *The closest cabins also look empty. No doubt their inhabitants are off on the beach somewhere, or on boats in the lake. People who own places like this rarely spend time in them during the daylight hours.*

She glanced nervously at her watch. *It's getting close to five in the afternoon. What if people start to drive home and notice me in the driveway? What if someone asks me what I'm doing here? What am I going to say? Waiting for an old boyfriend? Who may or may not show up?*

She hurried back into the car and sat down. She was glad that no one seemed to be around to see her, but she was still unsure as to what to do next. *If I still had a phone number for him, I could call and ask him to meet me here. Ah, no. I left my phone back in the limo. Anyway, he might not even talk to me. I'm right back to where I started at yesterday. No one loves me enough to care what happens to me.*

As she leaned the seat back to a more reclining position, she felt herself starting to cry again. She tried to fight the tears but realized that it didn't matter anymore. There was no one to see—no one to care—no one to turn to. She might as well cry to relieve her stress, because no one was going to show up to rescue her. Maybe she'd be able to think more clearly once she had a good cry.

She felt the tears roll down her face for a while, before a sense of immeasurable tiredness crept into her body. Overcome by the heat of the late afternoon sun, the fresh lake breezes, and the sleep deprivation she had experienced for weeks due to anxiety, she turned her head to a more comfortable position and drifted off into a deep sleep.

Eric wasn't sure what he was hoping for as he turned off the highway, heading down the back roads that led to the family cabin he and his brother had inherited. They had made extra keys for their cousins on their Mom's side of the family, all of whom lived out of state. But they were the principal owners, responsible for the upkeep and the taxes. And they were the ones who kept their personal belongings there, who kept the fridge stocked with beer and food, and the ones who took turns spending any vacation time they got in the one place they could truly relax in—their home away from home.

Was he hoping to find the place deserted? That would allow for him to have a relaxing weekend—sleeping late and looking at the bikini-clad girls on the beaches. Or did he want her to be there? With all that would mean? He would have to listen to her talk about the man she had almost married, and the reasons that she had run away from him. And he would vacillate between insane jealousy of the man who had recently been having sex with her—and a vague feeling of superiority that she had run *to* him this time, not away from him.

But what would that *really* mean? If she ran *to* him, did that mean that she wanted to see him? That she missed him? That she would finally admit how much he meant to her? Or did it mean that she viewed him as a harmless eunuch, who would let her cry on his shoulder, then pat her awkwardly as she made up her mind to return to the lifestyle her mother had been grooming her for since birth?

And do I care? Eric pursed his lips as he made the last turn that led to the private driveway. *Of course I care. If I didn't, I wouldn't have driven ninety miles an hour to get here, so I could see if she still thinks of this place – of spending time with me – as her shelter from the storm.*

He looked with interest at the small car parked on the beach side of the cabin. It had Illinois plates – a hopeful sign. When he got close enough, he peered inside. It appeared to have someone inside of it. *Asleep? With all of the noise that a Harley makes?* He was grinning as he pulled up to the other side of the cabin, parked, and turned the motor off. He got off the bike and stretched, his muscles cramped from riding for the past couple of hours. Jerkily he strode over to the car to examine it more closely. He saw her head lolled back, and heard, through the open windows, the sound of her snoring softly, but steadily enough to be heard over the sound of the lake.

So you did think of this place. And me. He almost chuckled with pleasure, before deciding against waking her up. He went around to the front door of the cabin and let himself in, to go in search of a cold beer to wash the dirt of the highway down his throat. He got some burgers out of the freezer to thaw for dinner, and spent some time thinking about what on earth he was going to say to her when she woke up.

CHAPTER SEVEN

Pamela moaned as she felt her excitement building. She was on her stomach, facing the bed, and being most gloriously pleasured by someone who really knew what he was doing. His hands were wrapped in her hair, and with strong, sure strokes, he withdrew, then entered her again, each time almost pushing her over the edge into screaming oblivion. She wriggled her ass appreciatively and felt him shudder. He regained control over himself, and the withdraw-enter rhythm resumed. She was so busy concentrating on her own feelings, that she didn't care who it was doing the work, as long as it continued.

This is a dream, but damn, what a great dream! I wonder who this fabulously satisfying man is? The realization that she was dreaming allowed her to take control of the action. Determinedly she pushed herself up, in order to turn around to see whose face she would be looking at — just who this mystery lover was that had her so hot that even in her dreams, she was dripping with heat and anticipation.

Reluctantly pausing while she turned over, the man bent his head down to lick, then suck at her nipples, one then the other, as she re-positioned herself under him. With an upwards thrust to her hips, she signaled her desire to be pleasured even more, with a full view of his face. He moaned, then thrust his hips forward to slam himself into her. Pamela fell over the edge into an extended multiple orgasm. Squeezing her eyes shut was the only way to concentrate on the feelings, to prolong them and make them more intense. She screamed as she rode the waves of pleasure, feeling herself clenching around the magic wand that this magician was wielding, feeling herself totally under his spell.

Finally she was able to breathe again, and she remembered that she was dreaming — and that his face was only inches from hers. All she had to do was open her eyes to see who the man of her dreams was. She opened her eyes to look at him. He raised his head, long black hair streaming down from his face in sweat-soaked strings, shadow of a beard darkening his face, and his blue eyes pierced through her heart. Eric? Even in my dreams?

With a start, Pamela sat up suddenly. The sound that had woken her up was being repeated, from close to where she was sitting. She concentrated and realized that the faint grating noise was a lock being opened, and the *thwack* that had woken her up was the sound of a window being pushed open. The cabin was no longer deserted. There was someone in it who was determined to let the fresh lake breezes in. She breathed a fervent prayer of supplication. *Please, dear God, let it be Eric, and not someone in his family whom I've never met. Please let it be Eric.*

She got out of the car, yawning and stretching. She walked slowly up the short walk to the front door to see if, despite her swearing in His house, God was in the mood to give her a break. Tentatively she knocked at the front door of the screened-in porch.

"I'll be right there!"

She smiled, breathing a quick, *Thank-you God*, as she waited for Eric to come to unlatch the screen door. She watched as he rounded the corner onto the porch. He stopped dead in his tracks when he saw who was at the door. Then he walked quickly over and opened the door. "To what do I owe this unexpected pleasure?"

Pamela smiled at him. "Aw, come on, you must have seen me sleeping in the car when you got here. You knew it was me, didn't you?"

As he pushed the screen door open, a slow smile crawled across his face.

"Yeah, I guess I did see a car with Illinois plates that I didn't recognize. So being a suspicious kind of guy, I looked in the window. And was I ever surprised! I asked myself, *Why is Mel here?* And then I remembered the news story that's being replayed over and over again, and I knew. You've run away again, and you need a place to hide out in for a while. Right?"

She gave him a defensive look. "Can't I just be visiting you? Since I haven't seen you in so long?"

"Bull shit, Mel! You're using me as a safe haven again, aren't you? Admit it—then maybe I'll let you stay."

She didn't realize that her lower lip was trembling as she turned to look at him. But he did. She saw on his face that he was having some kind of internal struggle with himself. She tried to influence him in her favor.

"You will? You'll let me stay her for a couple of days? Really?"

He nodded. "Yeah, sure. You can tell me all about why you ran away *this* time, and I'll be sympathetic. It'll make me feel good knowing that I'm not the only man you've run away from."

She shot him a reproachful look. "That was totally different, and you know it."

"Which time?" The sarcasm in his voice was extra heavy.

That stung. She looked away and grimaced, before turning to him hopefully. "Is there any beer in the cabin? I'm really thirsty!"

"Of course. Why don't you grab two of them, and bring them out here? Then you can tell me all about why you are *the runaway bride.*"

She gave him a questioning look.

"Hey, I didn't make it up. It's what the newscasters are calling you, now that the story is getting old. Obviously, someone is pushing for it to still be repeated, since they haven't found you yet. The talking heads are probably trying to give it a different spin, so it's not just old news."

Pamela nodded and turned to go into the house. She walked quickly into the kitchen to check out the beer selection, before grabbing a couple of Leinenkugel Summer Shandies from the fridge. When she got back out to the porch, Eric was sitting in one of the comfortable wicker chairs, his bare feet up on the coffee table in front of him.

Pamela handed him a bottle then sat in the chair facing his. He had the view of the beach and the lake, and she was looking at him, and into the hallway beyond his head. She twisted the top off of the bottle and took a long drink, enjoying the feel of the cold, slightly lemony bubbly brew, as it eased her dry mouth, and hopefully, her nervousness at being here with him again after so long apart. She kicked off her sandals and put her feet up on the table also, breathing out a long sigh of relief. "Ahh, does *this* feel good!"

He watched her from across the room. There was silence for a few moments. Eric cleared his throat. "So? Why did you run away and leave him at the altar?"

She shrugged. "It's kind of a long story."

He shrugged also. "We've got time."

Pamela sighed. "It's just that he never makes me feel important. See, he's trying to make full partner at his law firm, and he acts like that's the most important thing in the world. I guess he loves me. He's told me he does. But I just wanted to have one day—just one day, where he turns off all of his bullshit techie crap and pays attention only to me!"

"So he kept his cell phone with him, is that it? He took a call before the ceremony while in the church, and you got pissed?"

Pamela took a big gulp of her beer, belched loudly, then leaned forward. "No! That asshole had his blue tooth *in his ear while* I was walking down the aisle. One minute he's gazing into my eyes, looking like he thinks I'm the most beautiful woman in the world. The next, he's turning away from me to answer his fucking phone call!"

Eric raised both eyebrows. "*While* he was standing at the altar? During the ceremony?"

Pamela nodded, then leaned back in her chair dejectedly. "Yes. I hissed at him that he better not be on the phone, but he turned so that I couldn't see the front of him at all. Then when I got closer to him, I saw that he was talking, and I flipped out. I started to swear at him, and the people sitting closest to the altar got shocked at my choice of words in a house of God."

Eric smirked. "Yeah. You've always looked like butter wouldn't melt in your mouth, but you can swear like a marine!"

She grinned him.

"One of the things, I might add, that I've always liked about you. That—and the belching."

She smiled more broadly. "And I'll bet you can think of other stuff that you like about me, too."

Eric stiffened. The smile left his face and his eyes grew cloudy with emotion. He turned away from her to gaze out at the beach. "We aren't going to talk about that now."

There was another, longer silence, as Pamela wondered how she could apologize for having changed the mood of the conversation. She could feel herself becoming more aroused each minute she was alone with Eric again, and so close to him that she could see his heartbeat speeding up as the blood pulsed through the vein in the side of his neck. She hoped that he was fighting against the same desire that she was—wanting to strip naked and roll around on the porch floor. She waited.

Finally he looked back at her. "I still don't understand why you ran. This is everything your mother has wanted for you since she popped out a girl. This is what she has been grooming you for—marriage to a rich, ambitious player like your father."

Pamela nodded. "Yeah, I know. She's been coaching me through all of the shit leading up to the ceremony. She designed my dress, had it made at a fashion house, then bullied the seamstress into making a similar dress for her in a different color for half-price. She picked out the hairstyle and the stylist who did it, as well as the make-up guy who did us both. She's been doing everything she can to make this go smoothly. She's going to kill me when she sees me again."

Pamela got up and paced back and forth a few times. "That's why I just can't go home yet. I have to feel stronger before I face her, to try to explain myself."

"And what're you going to be explaining? Why you left? Why you want the wedding postponed? Isn't the groom the one you should be worried about facing?"

Pamela stopped pacing to gaze unseeingly at the lake. While she did, she could feel Eric's gaze on her. But her thoughts were in turmoil. It was his turn to wait.

With a sigh, Pamela turned and went back to the chair she had vacated. "See, the thing is, I'm not even sure I want to marry him anymore. I mean, if this is how he honors his promises to me *before* we're married, what's he going to be like *after* we are?"

Eric met her eyes steadily. "Probably more of the same. But by the time you are getting fed up enough to act on it, you'll have a couple of kids and you'll have them to think about also. If he knows you at all, he'll know how important family is to you. He'll be banking on your not wanting to break up their home, so he'll figure you will stay put. And your mom will back him up. She'll quote you statistics about children of divorced parents and try to make you feel guilty enough to stay with him."

Pamela nodded sadly. "Yeah, you're right." She leaned

forward with her forearms on her knees. "But you have a kid and you're divorced. He's doing okay, right?"

Eric's face was grim as he spoke in clipped, angry tones. "Diane *did* tell you all about me, didn't she? I'll bet she gave it an extra nasty spin too. Next time that bitch brings her car in, I'm gonna spit into the oil."

Pamela shook her head. "She just told me that you got married because you got someone pregnant, and that it didn't last much past the baby being born. I was surprised because you have always been so adamant about using condoms."

Her voice trailed off, as his face changed.

There was a mixture of anger and self-loathing on his face, as he looked past her, at the lake. "Not that you care, but it was after I tried to get you to tell your parents you were still seeing me. It took everything I had to send you away. But I was sick and tired of you coming back to see me whenever you felt like it, then leaving again, as if you were ashamed to have anyone find out that I was a part of your life. I guess I wanted you to have to make a choice once and for all. That didn't work out the way I hoped it would."

Pamela stared at him steadily but said nothing.

"After I realized what I had done, and that you probably weren't ever coming back, I went on a bender and drank *way too much* for a while. I even made a point of driving home drunk every night, because nothing mattered anymore. During that time I hooked up with a waitress at a bar. I was surprised the first time I woke up next to her, because I had never even noticed her before. I saw her a coupla times after that, because I was drinking way too much to care about anything. When I stopped going to that bar, I stopped seeing her. But she called me a month later and told me she was pregnant. I offered to pay for an abortion, but she didn't want one. So we talked about it and decided to get married, to give the kid a home. It was a really bad decision, but I wasn't thinking straight at the time."

His voice now changed to one filled with regret. "We were incompatible from the get-go. She's into country music and watching reality TV. I like blues and jazz, and I don't even own a TV. I read sci-fi books—she thinks anything more complex than a *TV Guide* is too hard to read. If I didn't have a son with her, I'd never want to see her again. But it's not his fault that his dad was a drunken asshole that one night. He deserves to have two parents who love him. So I see him when I can. Visitation rights are that I get him two weekends of the month, and for a month in the summer. We alternate the Christmas/New Year holidays."

"How old is he?"

Eric's face softened as he remembered his son, answering her with a smile. "He's two years old. He's kind of shy, doesn't talk much yet. But he loves it when I read to him."

"What's his name?"

"Jonathan."

"After your dad, huh?"

Eric nodded.

"When did he die, anyway? And why didn't you call me?"

Eric snorted. "What for? So you could say, *Sorry to hear about that. But I'm too busy with my life right now, to do more than send a card?*"

Pamela shook her head. "You know I wouldn't have said that. I'd have dropped everything to be by your side. Like I did when your mom died."

"That was when we were still in high school. We were dating then. You were helping me cope because you were my girl. You haven't been my girl for years."

There was an uncomfortable silence for a moment.

Eric sighed. "It was about three years ago. Right after I tried to make you choose. I was feeling insecure because I knew he was close to dying. I thought if I could get you to choose me, I'd be more emotionally secure—better able to handle his death."

He turned away from her to look out at the beach again for a few minutes. "I don't have any idea what you would have said. I don't even know you anymore. We've got separate lives now, Mel. I've got an ex-wife and a son. You've got a fiancé who is scouring the earth looking for you. And your parents are on his side. I've got no right to have any kind of opinion about you at all."

Eric looked surprised, as a single tear dropped down onto Pamela's hand.

She shook her head impatiently. "I need another beer. How about you?"

He nodded. "You go get them out of the fridge. I'm gonna go out and put the coals on for dinner. We can make some burgers and eat out on the beach. Why don't you see what else there is in the kitchen, for us to have with the burgers?"

"Then can we have a campfire and watch the sun go down? Like we used to?"

Eric smiled at her. "That's my plan, babe."

She nodded and got up.

They went separate ways to facilitate dinner.

While she was in the kitchen, Pamela found some buns and an unopened bag of chips. She poked around in the fridge while getting another couple of beers out, and found an onion, lettuce, a tomato, and some pickles. There was also an opened jar of *habañero salsa* that she put onto the counter, along with some taco chips that were in an already-opened bag on top of the fridge.

Eric came back in, smelling of smoke, and sat on one of the bar-stool-type chairs at the counter.

Pamela bustled around getting things sliced and ready for them to eat. They both munched on the chips and salsa as they drank their beer, waiting for the coals to be ready. They got everything they would need, including plates, onto a big round serving tray. Pamela carried the tray out.

Eric followed her carrying the plate with the raw burgers, and a small cooler they had loaded with a few more beers and some ice.

They chatted over the news of the day but avoided politics. Instead they spent some time arguing over their opinions of recent sci-fi movies and TV shows, while they made and ate dinner. When they were done, Pamela carried everything back into the cabin on the serving tray, while Eric brought a load of wood over from a pile under the extension of the roof that served as a breeze-way for sitting under during rain, or a pseudo-garage for anyone worried about leaving their car out during inclement weather.

By the time Pamela was done with the few dishes, Eric had a huge bonfire going. Pamela sat down next to him on one of the reclining beach chairs, and they toasted to each other with their newly opened beers.

"To peace and quiet."

Pamela smiled at him. "And to having a place to run away to—and someone who will take me in when I need him to."

Eric gave her an intense look before looking away, towards the lake. "Quiet now. We don't want to miss any of the sunset."

She smiled. He always said that on their previous trips to the cabin also. She was amused at his insistence that you could *see* better with silence. But as she also gazed at the changing colors in the sky, she felt a new appreciation for the quiet. Her mind cleared of all stress and worry, and she felt a sense of calm and peace, as she watched the miracle of a perfect sunset, in a comfortable chair, in front of a warm campfire, with one of her best friends sitting next to her. She took a few deep breaths and let them out slowly.

When the sun had finally disappeared behind the horizon of the lake, Pamela let out a long sigh. "That was truly beautiful. I had forgotten how magical it is to watch a sunset from your beach. Thanks for letting me share it with you."

Eric got up to toss another couple of logs onto the fire. He sat back down and turned to Pamela, speaking slowly, trying not to let his feelings show in his words. "So, what are you going to do now, Mel?"

She smiled at him, speaking hopefully. "Stay the night with you?"

He spoke sharply. "You can stay the night, but not *with* me. You'll be sleeping in one of the bunk beds in the kids' room."

Dismay flashed across her face. "I will?"

"Yes."

"Why?"

He exploded. "Because you *can't* keep on doing this to me, Mel! I'm not just your *ace in the hole*. Anytime you get into trouble, or you feel stressed by the life your parents want for you, you come running back to me. I have always taken you back, because I love you. Always have. Probably always will. But I have to love myself too. I have to protect myself from pain. I can't keep letting you give me another taste of paradise, before you run back to your *real life* again. I'm left feeling even emptier than I did before you returned. You used me like that for years and I'm tired of it." Abruptly he looked away from her, out at the dark sky. When he spoke again it was almost a whisper. "I'm not sure what hurts more, Mel—when you *don't* come to see me—or when you *do*, because I know how empty I'll feel when you leave me again."

Pamela felt tears squeeze themselves out of the corners of her eyes, but she brushed them away impatiently, hoping that he didn't see them. She spoke defensively. "I don't just use you. I—I guess I thought we meant enough to each other that you were always happy to see me. You always acted like it."

Eric's voice dripped with a pain she had never heard before. "Yeah. I'm happy to see you because I always think that maybe *this* time you came back because you have finally realized what we mean to each other. But that's never it. You come to see me. I don't ask about what caused you to run away this time. Being with you reminds me why I can't stop thinking about you even when I'm with other women. And then you leave me again—and I'm alone."

She was crying now, sobbing silently, listening to the depth of emotion in his words.

He spoke in hushed tones, as if he were afraid to speak any louder. "I can't take it anymore, Mel. Every time you come back, losing you is harder than the last time. Even that first time, when you left for college, it damn near killed me. Then you started sneaking away from your parents whenever you got a break and came home, and I would feel special because you were coming back to me. But that happened less and less as time went on. I knew you were busy with your classes, but I would torture myself, imagining how many men you were with—thinking that they were better for you, since they were going to college just like you."

He took a long drink from his beer. "Then you would come back again, and I'd be thrilled that you still wanted *me*. When you graduated and opened your practice, I hoped you would finally be ready to include me in your life. That's why I tried to get you to make a choice. But you stopped coming to see me after that—until the reunion. Dad had passed away by then, and I had no one to help me deal with that except for my brother—and he had his family. I felt really alone. And I was pissed about the bad choices I had made. I blamed you for them. That's why I rejected you when you came into the shop."

When Pamela spoke, her voice was shaking with emotion. "I could tell you were mad at me, and I couldn't figure out what I had done to deserve that. Oh Eric, I'm so sorry. I'm sorry I wasn't there for you when you needed me. I'm sorry you have felt so used. I really *do* care about you. You know that, don't you?"

He shook his head. "I don't know anything about you anymore, Mel. You have a fiancé now. You have an entire city looking for you. And you have to decide once and for all, what you want out of life. Not what your parents want for you. Or what your mother thinks you should want. What *you* want. I can't help you do that. No one can. It's up to you to choose."

Pamela spoke in a whisper. "What if I don't know what I want?"

Eric got up and finished his beer.

Pamela watched him, admiring his silhouette in the moonlight—the strong lines of his broad shoulders narrowing to his slim hips.

"You're not getting any younger, babe. You'd better spend some time thinking about that. I'm tired. I had a long day at work. I'm going to bed."

He turned and began to walk slowly up the path to the cabin. He stopped half-way up and turned back to her.

Her heart sped up, but his words quashed her hopes.

"Make sure the fire's out, and bank the coals before you come in. Good night."

She sank dejectedly back into her chair, staring moodily at the fire. *Great. Just great. How am I supposed to make any kind of decision, when he leaves me out here by myself? What am I supposed to think about?* She poked at the fire, moving the logs around to throw more heat back at her, then sat back in the chair and took a long drink from her beer.

Donald wouldn't leave me alone like this. He'd be all over me like fleas on a dog, convincing me that my place is in his bed. She thought about what sex with Donald was like. Sometimes it was prolonged, but more usually it was done quickly, like she was just another item to check off his agenda for the day. He was always willing to have sex, but insisted on keeping his phone on the nightstand where he could check it if it signaled he had a call or a text. More than once he had angered her by answering it *while* they were naked and getting busy. *That one time I stomped into the next room and refused to let him talk me back into bed when he was done with his call. The next day, a dozen roses were delivered to my practice, along with an invitation to dinner at one of the ritziest restaurants in downtown Chicago. Donald proposed after dinner, with the ring delivered in a glass that the waiter brought to our table, along with a bottle of Dom Perignon.*

I'll bet that Eric has never even had champagne, let alone Dom Perignon. What would he have a ring brought to the table in? An iced beer mug? Instantly she felt like a snob. She heard her mother's voice in her head telling her she deserved to live like a queen. She rejected it, like she always did to her mother's face. *No. I'm not like that. I don't care how much money Eric makes. We have a connection — we go way back together.*

Moodily, she settled back in her chair and remembered how they had met. And their shared history.

CHAPTER EIGHT

Pamela was pleased when her friend Diane sat with her at lunch. Some of the other girls were nice to her in class, but mindful of the stigma of being seen with her in public, they sat with each other at lunch—not at her table. Not only was she one of the only Black girls in the very expensive high school her parents had chosen for her, she was also older than the other girls. Her birthday was in early September, so she'd had to wait until she was six before she could start kindergarten. So even at the start of her senior year, she was already 18, and legally an adult. Which didn't make her hurt any less when she was ignored.

Diane grinned as she sat down, before leaning forward conspiratorially. "How would you like to ditch school with us tomorrow, and go to the beach?"

Pamela's eyes opened wide. "Uh—I don't know. Isn't there a chem test tomorrow?"

Diane shook her head. "No, remember? Old lady Shaker moved it to Friday, to give everyone time to meet with her, to go over their grades and any questions they have on the material." Diane winked at her. "Besides, what do you care? You already have an A in her class. Even if you do poorly on the test, you'll still have the highest grade in the class."

"Yes, I know."

"Come on, Pam. You never get asked to parties. You don't even have a boyfriend. I'm asking you now. Come with us to the beach. We need one more girl."

Pamela's eyebrows rose. "Who else is going?"

"Susie, Patty and me."

"Was someone else supposed to go with you?"

"Honestly, you're so suspicious."

Pamela stared into Diane's eyes.

"Okay, yes. Debbie was supposed to go. But her mom found birth control pills in her purse, and she's been grounded for, like, the foreseeable future. Come on, Pam. There are going to be four guys there. We can all have our pick. Don't you want to have some fun?"

"Well—maybe. But how are you going to get there?"

Patty's borrowing her dad's car. Her parents are both out of town. The only ones home are Patty's older brothers. And they don't care what she does."

Pamela thought quickly. *I haven't gotten into any trouble lately. I haven't even run away for a while. Why shouldn't I go have a little fun?*

"Are you gonna come with us?"

Pamela nodded, a smile spreading across her face. "You know, I think I will. Mom's always telling me I should be having more fun, since it's my senior year and all. She thinks I spend too much time on my homework."

"From your grades, I'd have to say she's right. Not that there's anything wrong with that. But you're only gonna be a senior for a year. You need to be creating some memories to make you laugh when you're old. That's what my gramma is always telling me."

"So how is this going to work?

"Have your parents drop you off in front of school, like always. We'll meet up with Susie, then sneak to the Dunkin Donuts to wait for Patty. Be sure to bring your bathing suit and some sunscreen. Unless you don't need it?"

Pamela made a face. "Hey, just because I'm bi-racial doesn't mean I don't burn. I'm half-white, remember? And that half burns really easily."

"I didn't mean anything. I was just wondering and all. But

just so you know, we probably won't be getting home until after dark. And by then our parents will know we ditched."

"Maybe we should tell them we're practicing up for senior ditch day."

Diane laughed. "Yeah, that's right! And I'm glad you're coming with. Now there will be four boys and four girls. Sounds like a real party to me."

Pamela had trouble concentrating on her classwork for the rest of the day. But the knowledge that she had been included in on one of the escapades of Diane and her friends, a clique she'd been unable to gain access to, made her so happy she wasn't even worried about being grounded.

I haven't been grounded lately. And maybe I can finally get a real boyfriend. I'm so glad I got rid of my virginity over the summer, with that friend of Cousin Ralph, when we were up visiting them on Martha's Vineyard. He wanted to cross the color line, and I just wanted the first time to be over and done with. Last year when I heard the senior girls in the locker room talking about sex, they said that the first time was really gross, and it kind of hurt. But after that, you really enjoy it. Now that the first time is over and done with, I need to start having some real fun with a boyfriend of my own.

When school was finally over, she waited outside for her mom to pick her up. She looked up when a car drove by, beeping at her. She didn't recognize the car, but Diane was waving at her out of the passenger side. "See you tomorrow, Pam!" Diane gave her a thumb's up sign Pamela returned the sign with a grin.

Since she always did homework after dinner, Pamela excused herself to go up to her room. She took a long time figuring out what to bring to change into for the beach. She packed the clothing, her bathing suit, a towel, and sunscreen into her backpack. Since her bag was always stuffed full of books, she hid them under the bed. *Now as long as no one picks up my backpack, it looks the way it always does. I'm set. And I'll say a prayer asking for a sunny day, before I go to sleep.*

Once her mom dropped her off in front of the school, Pam searched for Diane. Finally she saw her, sitting with Susie, on a bench near the school grounds. She went over to join them. They waited until the bell had rung, before they snuck quickly away from school. When they got to the Dunkin Donuts, they took turns changing in the bathroom. Off went the boring school uniform, and on went the shorts and halter tops, guaranteed to draw attention from the boys they were going to meet. They barely had time to order their donuts and coffee, before Patty strolled in looking for them. She got herself some food also, then they piled into her daddy's Caddie and hit the highway.

"Warren Dunes, here we come!" Diane yelled out of the window, waving at passing truckers, who beeped to salute a car full of teenaged girls. Susie, riding shotgun, turned the radio on loud so they could all scream along with the songs. And Pamela hugged herself, feeling wicked, looking forward to finding out how much fun she could pack into one day.

The Michigan beach was crowded even though it was a weekday. It was an unusually warm day for September. Toddlers and small children were busy making sand creations everywhere they looked. The boys they were meeting had already set up a net for playing volleyball and waved at them to invite them over.

Pamela had never met any of them before and felt shy about meeting four hot guys at once, while she was wearing only her bikini top, with shorts over the bottom of the suit. She always felt insecure in a bathing suit. Her friends were mostly skinny white girls with barely-there curves. She was on the voluptuous side, with an ample butt that betrayed her genetics even better than her *café au lait* skin color. At least her breasts were also on the larger side, so she hoped it balanced out in the eyes of anyone looking at her.

At first, she tried not to stare at the boys with their lean, hard bodies, as they romped around in the sand playing volleyball. As she watched them, she tried to decide which one of them was the best-looking. She had just chosen the one with the long dark hair, when she heard Diane talking to the other girls, as they experimented with the best way to pose on their towels.

"See that one? With the long dark hair? His name is Eric. He's an army brat who just moved into the neighborhood over the summer. He's really into partying. He's got an older brother who buys for him, so he's the one who brought the beer. Peter, the blond guy, is the one I'm dating. He told me that the beer's in a cooler in the trunk of the car. There's no alcohol allowed on the beach, but when we go to make some food by the grills along the drive, we can sneak into the woods so we can't be seen from the road."

The boys ran back over to the girls, challenging them to run into the water. Pamela offered to stay with their things on the beach, while the others went swimming. She thought everyone was in the water, so was surprised when a shadow crossed her face, then a towel was thrown onto the sand next to her. She looked up in surprise to see that the boy with the long black hair had the bluest eyes she had ever seen. He sat down.

"Not into swimming?"

She shook her head. "Not right now. I'm working on my tan." She saw his smile, and felt her heart skip a beat at the admiration in his eyes.

"Why? You're already a beautiful color. And I really like that suit on you. You have one of the most awesome asses I have ever seen."

Pamela laughed. "Is that a come-on, mister? Or are you just thinking of *crossing the color line* and I look like a good choice for that?"

He smiled at her again, shaking his head. "I've been across

that line and back again already, sister. I've lived all over the world. Believe me, I don't pick a color. I pick a girl. And you are the most interesting girl I've seen on the beach today. You caught my eye when you walked up. I thought to myself, *Damn! That's one fine lady. I have got to meet her, as soon as I get a chance.* So I headed for the bathroom when the guys were talking about jumping into the lake with the girls. I was hoping you would still be here when I got out."

He turned to lie on his stomach, as she was doing. He propped himself up on his elbows and idly picked up sand and let it run through his fingers. "So, my name is Eric. What's yours, beautiful lady?"

She giggled. "Pamela."

"What's so funny, Pamela?"

"You. You're such a flatterer. I'll bet you get any girl you want, with lines like that."

He gave her a lopsided grin. "Sometimes. And sometimes they decide I'm too sketchy for them, and they run in the other direction. Which one are you going to do?"

She gave him a long, considering look over the top of her sunglasses. "I think I'm going to stay right here, if that's okay with you."

"Good." He leaned over and kissed her.

Pamela was unprepared for the electric shock that ran from her lips down to her toes, with a special emphasis on her private parts, which tingled with excitement. She opened her lips in surprise. Eric took advantage of that to slip his tongue delicately into her mouth, exploring her.

After a while, during which both began to breathe quicker, he drew back and smiled at the expectant look on her face, from her half-closed eyes, to her full lips that she licked gently. "Yum. I wondered what you would taste like. As good as you look. Was it good for you?"

She giggled again. "You really are a player, aren't you?"

"Does that bother you?"

She shook her head. "No. I'm definitely interested."

"Good. Then you're mine for the day, okay? The guys were talking about who was going to go after who when you all walked up. But I had already decided by then that you were mine. That all right with you?"

She nodded shyly.

"Okay then. Now that that's all settled, we can enjoy ourselves."

And they had. The rest of the day was spent exploring the beach, running up and down the dunes, and swimming. When they got hungry, they all piled into the two cars and drove to a picnic area to grill some food. They took turns sneaking two-by-two into the woods to furtively drink beers and make out. Then they returned to the beach to linger over rubbing sunscreen all over each other.

They hadn't left the beach until the sun was beginning to set. Pamela knew that she was going to get into major trouble when she got home. She was so late that there would be no way to explain away why she had been at school for so long. And doubtlessly the school would already have called her parents to report her absence. But she had enjoyed herself so much that she figured it was worth anything her parents would dish out.

Besides, she gave Eric her phone number during one of their groping sessions. No matter how long her parents grounded her for, the first time she could go out again, she was going to be with Eric. That knowledge made her toes curl with anticipation.

Eric called her the very next day. She was grounded for a week, so he asked her to go out with him the first Saturday night she was able to. He told her that he worked most week-nights, and on Saturdays during the day. But he was done on Saturday by four, so he would pick her up at her house at six. She gave him directions to her house, then proceeded to spend the whole time dreaming about what it would be like to do the nasty things she was imagining doing with him.

On the night of their first date, she spent hours deciding what to wear. She settled on capri jeans, a lacy cammie, and a sleeveless shirt over it, to cover her bra straps. She was trying to look sexy yet not slutty, so her parents wouldn't say, "You can't leave the house looking like that, young lady!" She tied her long, curly hair back in its usual ponytail.

When Eric arrived, he was dressed in jeans, a tee-shirt with a flannel shirt over it, and sandals. He was unfailingly polite to her parents, which impressed her father at least. He told them they were going out for dinner, then maybe to a movie. He promised to have her home by midnight, and to take good care of her.

When they were walking down the sidewalk to his car, she had to ask. "How the hell did you learn to *work* grown-ups so well?"

"When your dad is in the army, he raises you to speak a certain way to adults. And because I always had to, it comes easily. They can spot a phony from miles away, but I make it seem natural. And Mom tells me that you get treated better if people feel you respect them."

He opened the door of his car for her. "Besides, I want your parents to like me. It would not have gone over very well if I told them what I *really* plan on doing with their daughter to-night!" He gave her a wicked leer, before walking over to the driver's side. He got in and started the car.

"I was beginning to worry that I dreamed it all up!" she said, pouting. "You haven't even tried to kiss me!"

"Not while your parents can still see us."

He drove them the few blocks down to his high school parking lot, where he stopped the car, put it into park, and turned to reach for her. "Now, I need to touch you again before I explode!"

He roughly pulled her closer to him. His kiss was needy, but Pamela responded to his every touch. Soon they were both panting again, as they groped and rubbed, kissing and licking, touching forbidden places through clothes, both moaning their impatience at having to remain clothed.

Finally he pulled back from the kiss, leaning his forehead against hers. "We have a couple of hours to kill until it gets dark enough for us to go park somewhere." His voice sounded harsh from the passion that had darkened his eyes to a midnight blue. "So what do you like to eat?"

"You really *are* taking me out to dinner?"

"What do you think I am? A beast? The kind of guy who takes what I want, without even thinking of your needs? Of course I plan to feed you. Besides, I'm hungry too!" He winked at her. "And we'll both need energy for what I have in mind. I do have a job, you know, so I have money. I go out to eat a lot. Mom is too ill to cook anymore, and Dad just sits around and drinks, because when he's sober, he has to remember that she's dying from ovarian cancer."

All of a sudden the mood was darkened. Pamela gently patted his face, trying to think of words of comfort to share with someone she barely knew. He had told her about his mom while they were tanning on the beach. But knowing what he had to live with was different from knowing how to make him feel better.

"I'm sorry," was all she could come up with. "I honestly don't know what to say to help you feel better. But I can think of something that might distract you." She took his hand in hers, and placed it under her shirt, directly on her right breast, and was gratified by the look of surprise and pleasure in his eyes.

"That'll work!" He leaned over and kissed her again, tenderly. He pulled at the ribbon she'd tied her hair back with and fluffed out her hair. He put both of his hands in it, massaging her scalp, as he inhaled deeply.

Then they talked about where to go to eat. Since they both liked Mexican food, they headed over to a neighborhood he knew about, where the store signs were all in Spanish. They enjoyed getting to know each other over taco chips, guaca-mole, salsa, and enchiladas. They were both surprised to dis-cover that Eric was already eighteen also. Since he had moved so many times with his family, he'd had to repeat first grade — he'd missed too many days of school, when his dad was sta-tioned out of the country, for it to count. They were not only surprised, but glad to discover that they had similar taste in music. And they both were sci-fi nerds — they dissected ar-cane points of some recent books and movies as they ate.

Since it was a sit-down restaurant, they were easily able to make their dinner, with appetizers, and after-dinner coffee, last two hours. When they finally made their way out of the restaurant, it was almost completely dark, and the moon was just visible over the horizon. They looked at each other and smiled. Eric pulled her into a strong embrace, crushing her to him, bruising her mouth with the intensity of his kiss, letting her know that it was time for them to go find a dark place and do all of the things they had both been imagining for days. He drove them to a nearby forest preserve.

"I've heard about this place, but I've never been here." Pamela wasn't sure what to make of the crooked half-smile that Eric gave her after she said that.

"I'm sure everything that you've heard is true. Kids aren't the only ones to know about it, though. The cops do too. If we're lucky, there will be some shift-changes going on, keep-ing them busy. Maybe there'll even be some big, like a DUI or a drug bust. As long as we get *some* time alone, I'm happy."

Eric parked in a dark area of a lot, far away from the street-lights, and near a copse of trees. He opened his door, walked around to hers, and helped her out of the car. He then opened the back door and gestured for her to precede him into the back seat.

"Considering what happens in the back seats of cars, you'd think they'd make them roomier and easier to move around in, wouldn't you?" Pamela was trying to cover up her sudden attack of nerves with small talk.

Eric's teeth gleamed in the early moon light. "That's why they don't. Don't want to encourage us. They want us all to abstain, remember?" He slid onto the seat beside her and pulled his door closed. He ran a hand over her curves, then put his other arm around the back of her shoulders, and leaned over to kiss her again, gently exploring at first, then more insistent, as she eagerly responded to his every touch.

They began to remove each other's clothing one piece at a time, laughing when the logistics of their movements was hampered by the close quarters in the car.

"Next time I'm bringing a blanket!" Eric swore, as he bumped his head on the roof of the car.

Once they were both naked, she nervously ran her hand over his now huge-looking engorged penis. "You *do* have a condom with you, right?"

"Yeah," he rasped. "More than one, in case we wanna go more than one round."

She smiled at the boxing image, then gasped as his fingers explored her wetness.

Eric drew in his breath with a low moan. "Girl, you are dripping wet! I guess that answers my question as to whether or not you really want this to happen."

"I wouldn't be here with you if I didn't." She started to squirm from the pleasant sensations she was getting from his probing finger. "Where's that rubber?"

"Eager beaver, huh?" He fumbled in the dark to dig the condom out of his pants pocket, which he first had to find.

"Yes." She helped him roll the condom onto his shaft,

grasping it at the base, to gently squeeze him, making him moan.

"That's enough of that!" he groaned. He pushed her back onto the seat, and leaned forward, grasping her hips. He slowly eased himself into her waiting body.

Pamela wasn't sure what she had expected — instant fireworks? Explosions? Pleasure beyond measure? After all, she wasn't a virgin anymore, so it didn't hurt this time. Instead she felt herself being opened and filled by him, and she leaned into it, trying to figure out how she was supposed to get any pleasure out of these awkward body movements.

As for Eric, his face was contorted with pleasure, as he moved himself gently in and out of her heat, kissing her face, her neck, one hand massaging her right breast, rubbing the nipple until she started to squirm without knowing why.

"Oh baby, you're so tight," he groaned. "So wet, so hot. I'm not gonna last much longer, if you keep moving around like that. Not — any — longer. Oh God!" Eric pushed himself into her one final time, then trembled with the intensity of his orgasm, his whole weight pushing her against the seat. Then he collapsed onto her, his head between her breasts, his hot breath blowing onto the nipple he had been fondling a moment ago.

When his breathing became more regular, Eric pulled back to a kneeling position in front of her and removed and tied off the condom, dropping it onto the floor of his car. He lifted his head up to look directly into her eyes. "That wasn't as good for you, was it?"

"No really, it was fine," she lied.

"You're not a virgin, but exactly how many times have you had sex?"

"Counting this one? Twice. But I haven't had many opportunities before. I go to an all-girls school you know. It's not for lack of trying." She sounded defensive and she knew it.

"Oh honey, I don't care about that," he answered her gently, as he twirled a lock of her hair around his finger. "But I can't leave you unsatisfied after you gave me such world-rocking, mind-blowing pleasure."

"I did?" she asked, thinking that he must be exaggerating.

"Oooh babe, yes you did! Now, what can I do to share this insane ecstasy with you?" His fingers began to trace a line over her body, lingering on her breasts, her nipples, then moving lower down. He bent his head to pull a nipple into his mouth. His lips and tongue made her squirm even more, trying for release from something she didn't understand. He sucked on the other nipple for a while, then began to lick his way down along her body.

She realized what he was planning on doing when he began to lick her belly button. She started to move.

He gently pushed her back onto the seat.

"No! I'm not sure I'm comfortable with you doing that."

"Why not? His head lazily dipped lower down, and he inhaled deeply, while his silky hair tickled her upper thighs.

"I don't know. Isn't it gross?" She disliked how shaky her voice was.

He smiled up at her, passion making his features softer, as his fingers traced where he planned to lick next. "No, you smell so good. Like you just had sex. With me. And are going to again. So sit back, relax, and enjoy the ride, babe."

He began to lick and lap at her, and she couldn't have moved if she had wanted to—and she certainly didn't want to anymore. Her legs felt like they were burning, and she squirmed her hips around, once again not even knowing why. But when her movements made him lick in different places, all of a sudden she realized why she kept moving her hips around. It was like her body knew what she wanted.

Pamela ran her fingers through her lover's hair and moaned, as he licked and sucked, and began to poke first one, then two fingers into her wetness again. She felt like she was getting onto a roller coaster, and the car kept on riding up and up a huge hill. The more he stroked her, the faster the ride got, until she gasped in amazement at her own impending orgasm. What had started as a minor feeling now began to feel like heat itself, as she realized that he was bringing her to the edge, then backing off, then bringing her up to the edge again. With a moan of frustration, she moved her hips once more.

Suddenly she had to squeeze her eyes shut at the explosions of light and color that she saw, while the roller coaster car dipped, then raced up another small hill, then dipped again, then raced up, then dipped, until she had no control over her own body, and she felt herself spasm repeatedly on his fingers and against his face. The world narrowed itself down to the feelings in her body as she had her first multiple orgasm. She vaguely realized that she heard screaming—it was her voice. She collapsed onto the seat finally. She opened her eyes to see Eric fumbling around for another condom.

"Can you breathe yet?" He looked immensely pleased with himself.

"Yes!" She gasped, then reached down to feel his once-again rock-hard erection. "Are we going to have sex again?"

"After you came so hard? Yeah."

He sat down on the seat next to her and pulled her onto his lap. "This time, you're on top, so you control the action. You're in charge of how deep I go—you pick the rhythm you want, and I'm just gonna enjoy the show. And hope you bring me along on that ride you were just on."

She put her knees on either side of his thighs and lowered herself onto him. This time the feeling was one of indescribable pleasure almost immediately. Her previous orgasms prepared her to enjoy feeling him inside of her, and all the practice she had done with Kegel exercises made her able to squeeze him with inner muscles that made him moan. They rocked and rolled together.

He reached down to hold her breasts, and dipped his head to suck at one nipple, then the other.

That made her muscles tighten even more and brought them both closer to the point they were trying to get to. She rocked back and forth on him, feeling him move himself, impaling her, moving so deeply inside of her, that she felt an odd sensation, as if he were coming to the end of her. Then she moved one more time and they both gasped, as she spiraled into orgasms again. She rode the roller coaster up and down, this time bringing him along with her. They both felt their body parts pulsing—his sperm testing the limits of the condom—her wetness running down her body onto his. They both moaned out their pleasure, as spasm after spasm shook them.

Feeling unable to even move, Pamela collapsed against Eric's chest, her head on his shoulder, her face mashed against his skin. She inhaled deeply, both because she needed the oxygen, and because she loved the smell of his skin up close. His hands rubbed her back, stroking gently down to the small of her back, then to the curves of her butt cheeks, holding on possessively.

When she could talk again, Pamela lifted her head up and looked adoringly at Eric. "That was really something, huh? Wow!"

He smiled lovingly back at her. "Like nothing I've ever experienced before, babe. You are wonderful!"

"How did you learn so much about how to please a woman?" She didn't want to move off him yet, wanting the mood to continue, in a warm bubble of sexual satisfaction.

He smiled. "I read a lot." He laughed as she made a face.

"Yeah, right!"

"No, really. My older brother gets *Playboy*, *Hustler*, all of that shit. I've been looking through them for years. But besides drooling over the pictures, I read all of the letters to the editor, with women answering questions written in by guys whose girlfriends are unsatisfied. I swore to myself a long time ago that if I ever met someone I really cared about, I'd be able to make her scream. I'm not rich, not that smart, not that good-looking. But I swear that no one else can give you pleasure the way that I just did!" He looked wickedly self-satisfied.

Pamela sighed with immense satisfaction. "No one else can please me like you can, you bad boy!"

"Bad boy? Puh-leeze. You ain't seen nothing yet, babe."

"You mean it can be better?"

"I told you I'm bringing a blanket next time. We need more room to spread out in. Then we can really get down to business."

He kissed her firmly, as if to seal the promise he had just made. Then he made motions for her to move.

"Do I have to?" Her lips pouted. "I like being on top of you!"

"We don't want the condom to slip off. Besides, it probably won't be much longer until the shift change for the cops. I really don't want our night ruined by getting busted for public nudity."

"We're not in public. We're in your car."

"That's parked in a public place. Let's get dressed. Then we can lie on the hood of my car and look at the stars, while we make plans for what we'll do the next time we can get together!"

They searched around for all the pieces of their clothing, finding some things in the front, some in the back, and even some hanging from the steering wheel. "See," he said pointing. "That's the kind of thing that gives away what's going on in the back seat. It's not cold enough for the windows to be fogged yet, but a bra hanging on the steering wheel just signals there's serious teenager mischief going on in this vehicle."

Pamela giggled as they finished dressing themselves. They got out of the back seat, to stand next to his car. Eric pressed her back against the passenger door and leaned into her, to kiss her thoroughly and deeply. Then he took her hand to lead her around to the front of the car. He picked her up by her hips and pushed her back onto the hood. He climbed up beside her and put his head onto her lap, to look up at the stars.

They spent a pleasant few minutes looking up at the stars, only to be blinded by the headlights of a car coming up the drive. They were not at all surprised when an officer jumped out of the car and crunched along the drive to shine a huge flashlight right into their faces.

"And what's going on up here with you two tonight?" The flashlight swept along their bodies, obviously looking for missing or open clothing.

"Nothing, Mr. Officer, sir," said Eric, once again in his *polite-to-adults* mode. "Just me and my girl, looking at the sky, hoping for a shooting star, so we can make a wish."

"Well, it's getting awful close to midnight, and that's curfew for you young folks. You'd best be getting this young lady on home to her parents."

"Yes sir, I'll be doing that right now, sir." Eric jumped down from the hood and solicitously helped Pamela down after him, carefully not touching her anywhere that might be misconstrued as cheeky by the watchful cop.

The officer peered closely at Pamela's face. "You look like a nice young lady. You shouldn't be spending your time alone with guys in a forest preserve. Boys like him might get the wrong idea about you."

She nodded meekly. "Yes sir."

Eric opened the door and she slid into the front seat, pointedly putting her seatbelt on immediately.

"Good night, sir," Eric said politely, before getting into the driver's seat, and fastening his seat belt also.

The policeman tipped his hat to them and watched as they drove away.

"Wow, you're good!" Pamela said, as she exploded into gales of laughter once they were out on the street. "Not only did you call it that he'd be coming, but you're so fucking polite that the only thing he could bitch about was how late it is!"

Eric joined in her laughter. "What an asshole! Like I said, next time I'll bring a blanket, but we'll go further into the woods. And I'll start scouting out other places, so we can have some privacy when we're together."

"We'll be together again?" Pamela asked in a small voice, trying not to sound as insecure as she felt.

Eric pulled the car over to the curb and put it into park, before pulling her across the seat, into the curve of his arms. "Every night that we can manage. You're *my* girl now, understand? Now that you've discovered that sex can be mind-blowing fun, I don't want you wandering off with every Tom and Dick that's hairy, in order to pleasure yourself, you hear? *I'm* the only one who gets to make you scream. Okay?" He tilted her head up with one finger under her chin and he kissed her again, deeply and with great feeling.

Pamela hummed with pleasure, trying unsuccessfully to ignore the insistent warmth that called to her again from her nether regions.

"You're sure there's no time for another quickie tonight?"

Eric smiled. "No, Mel, it's way too close to midnight. I don't want your parents to decide I'm not a good influence on their little girl. I promised to have you home by then, and I always keep my promises."

"Promise me that you'll stay my guy?" she boldly asked him.

He studied her seriously for a moment, before crossing his heart with his fingers. "Cross my heart and hope to die. And you?"

She crossed her heart also, as he had done. "Stick a needle in my eye, if I lie."

They kissed once again. The nearby church bells start to toll for midnight. Pamela slid back across the seat, and Eric drove them back to her house. He walked her back up to her door.

"Aren't you going to kiss me good-night?" she asked him, when he turned to leave.

"Won't your parents be watching?"

"Yeah, but I think it would be okay if you do. They're probably expecting it."

"I'm afraid they'll realize that we're lovers, since I won't be able to keep my hands off of your perfect ass."

She smiled up at him.

"I just want one more kiss, before I go to sleep and start to dream about you!"

"Okay." He bent his head down and kissed her. Even though it was much more of a chaste kiss than before, still Pamela felt her toes curl in her shoes.

"Good night, Eric," she said, as he turned to leave.

"Good night, *Pamela-who-belongs-to-me*," he answered with a wicked grin on his lips.

They heard the front door open. Eric waved at her parents, then turned and went whistling back to his car. Pamela went into the house and feigned great tiredness, so she could take a long, hot shower, then fall into bed to relive every moment of their night together.

"Tonight I really became a woman," she whispered to herself, as she began to drift off to sleep. Every muscle ache in her body reminded her that she was now *Pamela-who-belongs-to-Eric.*

Halloween was great fun. Pamela enjoyed being tarted up for the night, to show off for her man. Her breasts were pushed up in a padded bra, while she had on a skirt that was so short, she almost flashed her thong getting up from a chair. She had done some research based on what she had learned in her dance classes and had chosen to dress like an *Adagio-dancer*. She showed Eric pictures she had found, so he had dressed the part also. He was the French-looking guy with a drawn-on mustache and goatee, and a black beret. He tied his hair back, and wore tight black pants, with a striped shirt. They spent some time at her school dance, teaching everyone there how *dirty dancing* was meant to be done.

They were both so aroused they didn't even wait to get out of the parking lot. Pamela climbed on his lap in the back seat of his car. Eric moved the thong aside, slipped on a condom, and they steamed up the windows of his car before most of the people had even begun to leave the dance.

Thanksgiving was awkward since her parents invited Eric to join them. His mother was so ill, he asked if he could take a plate home for her. Pamela's mom had made up two plates, so his father could have some turkey and stuffing also. The conversation around the table was stilted, with Eric being un-failingly polite, and her parents trying to find out as much as they could about this boy who was dating their daughter.

It was obvious from the pointed questions her mother asked, that she didn't feel Eric was good enough for her little girl. Pamela worried that Eric would take offense from her mother being such a snob. When she walked him out to kiss him goodbye at his car door, she was worried that he might think she was as class-conscious as her mother.

"I'm not like her, you know. "I don't care how much money your parents have, or what kind of job you have. You know that, right?"

He laughed before kissing her thoroughly. "Mel, none of

us gets to pick our parents, and they don't get to pick us either. We're all stuck with what we get. Mine are truly much weirder than yours. Just be glad we got to eat here, instead of at my house."

Christmas was the best, since it meant a two-week vacation from school. They had lots of time to spend together, even though Eric worked more hours during his off time from school, than he did when they had classes. He was working at a service station, since he had both an aptitude, as well as an interest in learning how to work on cars. He had started by cleaning up after the mechanics. They soon realized what he already knew, and how eager he was to learn more. So he was encouraged to help in major ways.

He got a big raise right before Christmas, which allowed for so much gift-buying that Pamela felt guilty.

"Don't feel bad, babe. I'm having a blast watching you open everything."

She was touched by the gold heart locket. He showed her how to open it. He had already put his picture on the one side, and hers on the other. "So everyone can see how well we go together." To his delight, her grateful kisses were unrestrained.

January was a rough month for Eric, from the first week. His mother, who had been fighting her cancer for the past few years, finally succumbed to it, and he was at home with his father when she took her last breath. Pamela was unsure of how to comfort her man but made sure to be there whenever he seemed to need to talk. She had held him while he cried, murmuring comforting words of love.

They planned the memorial service together, since his dad completely fell apart, spiraling further into an alcohol-fueled fog once his wife was gone. Since they were new in town, there was no need for a big service. And since his mother was cremated, there was no wake to plan. But they arranged a luncheon at a local formal restaurant, and Eric's older brother drove in from the college he was attending in Michigan. A few of Eric's relatives from out-of-town managed to make it in for the day.

Pamela knew that it didn't matter to Eric that she didn't like to have sex during her time of the month. He insisted that even when they were not going to *get busy*, he still liked to spend time with her, since he considered her not only his girl-friend, but his best friend as well. So in keeping with that spirit, Pamela made herself accessible to him while he worked through the pain of losing his mom. They didn't do any actual dating during this time. They just spent time together, either quietly enjoying being with each other, or with him talking about how he felt. They took long walks in the cold, enjoying the sound of the snow crunching under their feet while they walked. Gradually, Eric began to find his way out of the misery of bereavement.

This meant that February, with Valentine's Day, was even more enjoyable for both of them. They exchanged cards and went out for dinner. For the big surprise, Eric snuck her into his house, and they got to enjoy each other in a real bed. His brother had supplied him with a six-pack of beer, and they giggled and enjoyed their mild buzz, while his Dad slept in the other end of the house. They had both fallen asleep after making love as quietly as they could. But Eric had the presence of mind to set his alarm clock. They woke up just in time for her to be home shortly after midnight.

March was the best month of all for their relationship. Diane was dating Pamela's cousin Bob. Pamela introduced them, so Diane told her that she owed her one. At lunch, when Diane told her that her family was going to Florida for spring break, she gave Pamela a significant look. "I told my mom that you'd be willing to keep an eye on our house for us, while we're gone. You can do things like bring in the mail every day.

Shovel the walkway if it snows. Water the plants." Then Diane winked at her. "Of course, we'll have to give you a key. You can use mine." She leaned closer to whisper. "Only use my bed and wash the sheets before we get back. Deal?"

That week was the first time that Pamela realized what being an adult must feel like. She would go over early in the afternoon, make some food, then Eric would join her when he got off work. They talked about their day, compared notes, ate companionably together. Then they would have wild monkey sex until they both passed out from sheer exhaustion. Even the non-sexual times were special, since they were able to lounge around naked, or with her wearing the lingerie which had been Eric's secret Valentine's Day gift to her. They totally enjoyed their time together.

The only fly in the ointment of her pleasure was that Pamela's parents were insisting that she actively pursue the colleges that she had chosen, to ensure being accepted, and to find out what kind of scholarship money she would be able to get. Whenever Pamela would talk to Eric about college, he got sullen and quiet. They both knew that his dad had no money to send him to college. His brother had earned a scholarship with his football skills and his grades, but Eric was going to be stuck at home, working at the service station while she went away. It was easy to ignore this when it seemed so far away. But as April ended and May began, the acceptance letters arrived, and Pamela had to finalize the decisions about where she was going. This was when the arguments started, and when the perfect love that Pamela and Eric had, began to sour.

Pamela was upset that Eric was trying to get her to study locally, since she still wanted to leave her parents' house. His half-hearted marriage proposal was way out of line, since she was not ready to take on that kind of commitment. She pointed out to him that she would be resentful, always wondering what her future might have been like, and that she didn't want to take the chance that she would live to regret having chosen to stay with him.

She sent him a card that had a picture of a butterfly on it, along with the words: *If you love something, set it free.*

If it doesn't return, it wasn't really yours to being with.

If it does, then embrace love, for you have found it.

This had done nothing to improve their relationship. By their graduation they were barely speaking to one another.

Then her parents had dropped a bombshell on her at her graduation party. They were putting the townhouse on the market, since once she moved out, they wouldn't have any kids living with them. Her mom and dad had already found a condo on the lakefront and signed the contract for it.

Eric got to the party late, so he wasn't there for the big announcement. Once Pamela told him about the move, he stormed out of the house, telling her, "There's no point to pretending anymore. You're leaving me, just like Mom did."

She tearfully pleaded with him to stay, to spend at least what little time they had left during the summer, together. But he told her to go ahead and get the hell out of his life.

They had a brief reconciliation in July, when they ran into each other at the Fourth of July fireworks. They were both so miserable apart that they agreed to not discuss anything that would make them fight again. During the month of July they tried to just be lovers. But every discussion every time they were together ended up being about how he didn't want her to go away, and how much she would miss him, but felt she had to go.

Finally in early August, he told her that he couldn't live under such emotional strain anymore. He had lost his mother, his father was unbearable to live with, and there was no way out of the hell his life had become. "We need to make a clean break. You're leaving soon, and I need time to get over you. But I'll tell you one thing, Mel. You're going to be sorry you let me go. No one will ever love you like I do. So go, live the life you were born to live. Bye."

Pamela went to her out-of-state college but missed Eric from the start. When she was back visiting her parents at Christmas, she called him and lied to her parents about where she was going. Their passion was explosive, their lovemaking frenzied, as they both tried to express without words what they felt for each other. All too soon break was over, and Pamela headed back to her college.

This pattern continued for years, with stolen moments spent together whenever Pamela could get away. She knew that her parents would not approve if they realized that she was still seeing the man they thought wasn't good enough for their daughter. But whenever she was feeling particularly needy, all she had to do was get back to the city, whether or not her parents knew she was around, and she would stay with Eric until the last minute. Even her closest friends didn't realize that she was still seeing him.

Eric sometimes accused her of keeping their relationship a secret because she was ashamed of him. Pamela tried to appease him, saying that since their relationship was only between the two of them, it was no one else's business. She always regarded him as her secret *security*, since she knew he would always take her in, no matter the reason for her needing to be with him. Things went along like that until after she graduated from veterinary school. When Eric told her she had to either tell her parents about their continuing relationship or end it, she had run away from him, telling herself she needed time to think it over.

Her mother distracted her with constant introductions to other men, and Pamela told herself it was for the best. *So what if no other guys ever seemed to be able to measure up in my eyes to Eric? Each time I reject a guy, Mom sets me up with another one.* She had just started dating Donald when she got the invitation to the reunion. Curiosity had gotten the better of her, and she wanted to go just to see Eric again — to see if there was still anything between them. When Eric rejected her overtures, she was shocked.

Shaken by his pulling the rug out from underneath her, by refusing to be with her when it was convenient for her, she had run back to her rich boyfriend, determined to show Eric that if he didn't care about her anymore, then she didn't care about him either.

Pamela sighed heavily as she drained the last drop of beer out of the last cold bottle she found in the cooler. "Okay Eric. I've thought about it. But I still don't know what I really want. Except I do know that I want you. I need you. But you told me to sleep in a bunk bed. So do I disobey you and hope that you forgive me?"

She shuddered as she remembered the pain in his voice, as he told her how much she had hurt him over the years. "Oh Eric, why didn't you tell me this before? I thought it was a good thing for both of us. I had no idea you felt so used. Or that I hurt you so much."

With another long sigh, she used the nearby shovel to put ashes over the embers that were still smoking. Then she got up and stretched before picking up the cooler to carry it back up the path to the cabin. She walked onto the porch and went into the kitchen. She stood still for a long moment, as she tried to decide where she was going to sleep for the night.

She heard Eric snoring, then shrugged. *I guess you're not up for anything tonight. Maybe not with me ever again.*

Now totally depressed, she went into the bathroom to quickly wash her face before stumbling in the dark to the kids' room with the bunk beds. She pulled off her tee-shirt and her shorts and fell into the bottom bunk on the side closest to where she could hear Eric snoring. She briefly wondered how she was going to be able to get any sleep at all, before her extreme tiredness caught up with her. She fell into a deep and dreamless sleep.

Chapter Nine

Pamela was moaning in her sleep, dreaming about wild sex with a half-human alien with long black hair, when a grinding noise interrupted her mood. She opened her eyes to realize she was hearing a coffee grinder. She was momentarily confused as to where she was. Gradually she remembered, and realized she was hearing breakfast being prepared. She heard the coffeemaker brewing, and that smell alone made her want to get out of bed.

She smelled bacon also, and heard eggs being cracked on the side of a bowl. She remembered that Eric had always been particularly proud of his omelet-making abilities. So she got up and padded barefoot into the kitchen.

Eric glanced up briefly when she walked into the kitchen. The sudden look of naked lust on his face reminded her that she was only wearing her underwear.

"Um, do I have time for a shower?"

He had quickly looked back down at the food he was preparing, but he nodded. "I guess so. But make it quick. I figured we'd head out to the beach. We're not that far from Warren Dunes, and I haven't been there in years. We can go race each other up the dunes, to see which one of us is showing our age. What do you think of that idea?"

"Ha-ha. Bring it, boy. I'm up for it." She furrowed her brow. "But I don't have a bathing suit with me."

"Do you have anything you can wear swimming? My sister-in-law doesn't usually leave much clothes around here. Plus she's had a few kids, so she's not in the kind of shape that you are." There was admiration in his voice, as his eyes fixated on the nipples poking through her bra in the early morning chill.

"Um—I have an exercise bra with me, so I can wear that on the top. And I also have a pair of short shorts, so I guess I can wear that on the bottom."

"Then get a move on, girl. The omelet is going into the pan in a minute. You'll want to be done soon, so you can eat it while it's hot."

She nodded and went onto the porch to grab her bag, before heading into the bathroom for a quick shower.

Once he could hear the shower water, Eric grabbed the side of the counter to steady himself, taking a series of deep breaths, and counting to ten very slowly. *Oh my fucking God! No woman should look that good when they wake up. She's in my shower, naked. Give me strength, Lord. Make me strong enough to wait until she's made up her mind.*

He busied himself cracking more eggs and poured the mixture into the pan. By the time Pamela was out of the shower, he had put the cover onto the pan, to melt the cheese. He turned to pour her a cup of coffee.

Pamela poured herself a small glass of OJ from the carton on the counter and perched on one of the chairs.

"Are we eating in here, or on the porch?"

"The porch—the view is nicer."

"Okay, I'll bring some of the stuff out there now."

She carried the juice carton, two glasses, and a pile of napkins onto the porch, setting them all on the coffee table they had rested their feet on the night before. She looked around and sighed with pleasure at the comfortable surroundings, with a fabulous view of Lake Michigan.

"Hey Mel. Come on back and get your plate and your coffee."

She turned and went back into the kitchen, where Eric thrust a plate into her hands. She grabbed the coffee he had poured for her, along with the salt and pepper shakers. He brought his plate, his coffee, and the jar of salsa. They both sat in the chairs they had used the day before, enjoying their breakfast, making comfortable small talk as they ate. Eric had left the CD player on in the kitchen, and they both smiled when songs they had enjoyed when they were in high school came on, bringing memories with them.

"That's the first song we danced to together," Pamela noted.

Eric nodded. "Uh-huh, I remember. I kept stepping on your toes."

They both grinned at the memory.

"Yeah, but I was paying so much attention to you in those tight pants, that I didn't care if you broke all of my toes. All I could think of was getting my hands on you."

Eric took a sip of his coffee, then put the cup down to look into her eyes. "Did you think about what I said last night?"

Pamela nodded.

"Did you come to any decision?"

Pamela sighed. "I'm not sure. But I did do a whole lot of thinking. And I had a good night's sleep. I feel a whole lot better than I did yesterday."

"The air is cleaner close to the lake. And there's the sound of the tide on the beach all night. That always relaxes me."

"So now what?"

Eric smiled at her. "You do the dishes, since I cooked. I'll take a shower. We can pack what we need to take to the beach before we head on out to spend the day baking in the sun. Sound good to you?"

Pamela nodded. "Sounds like a plan."

"Excellent. Then let's *make it so*."

They both smiled at his indulging his inner sci-fi nerd self with his *Star Trek* reference. Eric carried his dishes into the kitchen, then headed for the shower. Pamela finished the dishes quickly, then started to hunt in the fridge for food to bring with to the beach. Eric joined her in the kitchen to pack. They were both hyper-award of their close physical proximity, but neither wanted to acknowledge their discomfort out loud.

"What should we bring with us?"

Eric reached into the freezer and pulled out a baggie.

"I've got some brats here. Bought 'em in Wisconsin the last time I was camping up there. Boiled 'em in beer last time I was out here. They'll be ready for the grill by the time we are hungry enough to care. Are there any buns left?"

Pamela nodded. "Yeah, as long as you don't mind burger-shaped buns. There's another onion and tomato too. And mustard. And another bag of chips."

Eric rinsed out the cooler before pulling a bag of ice out of the freezer to dump into it.

"We'll have to stop along the way to get more beer and ice. I guess we should take your car instead of my hog, huh?"

"Unless you plan on me balancing the cooler on my head with one hand, while I hold onto you with the other. Yeah, we can take the car. I rented it for the weekend. I have to bring it back tomorrow."

"Good. We can throw the cooler and the towels and stuff into the trunk. That way we can hide the beer under a blanket until we get into the park."

"So, are we all packed?"

They had been getting things into the cooler or bags while they talked, so Eric nodded as he looked around. "I'm forgetting something—oh yeah, my Frisbee."

He went quickly into the master bedroom, to re-emerge smiling, tossing the disc into the air and catching it with the same hand.

"That's the same one you had with you the day we met?"

Eric smiled. "Yup."

Pamela smiled back at him. "I've got a really good feeling about today."

Eric nodded. "Me too. Let's get this show on the road."

A little over an hour later, Pamela got into the line of cars waiting to get into the park. Since it was early on a Sunday, they didn't have too long to wait before they were driving along the access road into the park. She drove until the road ended in a series of parking lots.

"Park in the furthest one, like we did before," Eric directed.

She drove to the remote lot, then parked in a spot close to the beach, under one of the few trees available.

They unloaded what they would need for a few hours, then headed down towards the less crowded areas of the beach. Walking barefooted in the shifting sands slowed them down, but they eventually got to a spot that Eric decided was far enough away from the families with little kids, so they wouldn't get sand thrown all over them, but close enough to the bathroom that it wasn't too far of a hike.

They put their towels on the beach and lay face-down, to begin working on their tans.

"Ah, this is the life," Eric said sometime later, as he rolled onto his back. He sat up to open a bottle of water and took a long swallow, trying not to stare, but unable to look away from the woman lying next to him. He knew that she disliked the shape of her body—most women did, for some strange reason. She felt that she was too big, too round, too curvy. She bemoaned her father's contribution to her genetics that made her taller than most females, with a large, attention-grabbing butt, and very generous curves. True, she didn't look like the skinny white girls she had gone to school with. But she never seemed to understand when he told her that he found everything about her to be wildly exciting.

He felt his heart lurch and his cock twitch, as his eyes

lingered over Pamela's curves while she lay next to him. She had the most exquisite shape to the small of her back that he had ever seen—leading to the sensuous curve of her upper buttocks. He got hard every time he remembered what it was like to see himself buried in her, while his hands roamed all over those luscious round globes. He was breathing quickly and sweating. It had less to do with the heat of the day, and more to do with the heat he felt for her. His hands trembled from their desire to touch her, and he was fighting hard against his own instincts.

"Hey Eric, can you rub some sunscreen on my back please? I don't feel like rolling over yet, and I don't want to burn."

He was undone. He swallowed hard. "Uh—okay. I guess. Where is it?"

She looked up at him and smiled. "Right there by the Frisbee, silly. What's wrong? Heat got to you already?"

He nodded. "Something like that." He squeezed the bottle over her back.

She squirmed and squealed. "That tickles!"

He leaned over and began to rub the lotion onto her skin. It took all his willpower not to trail his lips where his hands had been. He tried to concentrate on how bad sunscreen tasted, since he had found that out years ago on the beach with her. He shook his head. *I need a cold shower! Now!* "Hey Mel, I'm going to run into the lake to cool off a bit, okay?"

She nodded. "I'll be here. Thanks to you I won't be burned to a crisp when you get back."

He walked awkwardly out to the water's edge, his cock so hard he figured he could have pole-vaulted more easily. He was immensely glad they were not near any families with small children, whose heads would have been eye-level with what he was trying to hide. With relief, he threw himself face first into the water. He felt the immediate physical reaction that cold water caused on him, relieving the immense pressure that was making it impossible for him to think of anything else except tearing her clothes off and making her scream. *Jesus, that was close! Give me strength. Maybe bringing her out here wasn't such a good idea after all. But what was the alternative? Spending the day alone with her in the cabin, with all those beds available?*

He cut a swath back and forth in the water, using strong strokes to propel himself from one end of the cove they were in, to the other. He kept an eye on her, to be sure that no one was bothering her, but he stayed out swimming until he was exhausted, so he would be less likely to act on the feelings he knew would return the minute he was close to her again. And he agonized over how close he was to losing control over himself, and how much he wanted to touch the only woman he had ever loved.

Well, that didn't work. Pamela watched Eric run out to the lake after smearing sunscreen on her back. *How am I going to get him to admit what he feels for me is too hard to resist? What we both feel for each other? He knows why I ran to him — we both do. Because like he told me so long ago, no one has ever given me pleasure like he does.* She sighed heavily. *Oh Eric, don't fight it. Admit it. We belong together.*

Pamela sat up in shock. She felt her heart race, and her hands shook as she reached for the bottle of water he had opened. She swallowed quickly, then put the bottle down and curled her knees up under her chin. She watched as Eric swam with a powerful stroke, back and forth, keeping an eye on her, but obviously trying to tire himself out. *Is that what you wanted me to think about last night, Eric? I know that — I've always known that. But I don't know if I have the strength to face my parents and tell them that. They have such high hopes for me — other plans. No one ever asks me what I want. They tell me what's best for me.*

Eric came running back up the beach and shook himself over her, like an over-sized dog.

"You jerk! That's cold!" She jumped up to push at him, and he laughed and danced backwards out of her reach. She chased him, and he ran back into the water. She followed him and they splashed each other and pushed, until Pamela went backwards into the water and came up spluttering and coughing, to spit out what she had swallowed.

"You okay?" Eric was solicitously by her side, his hands on her shoulders, when she gave him a hard push and he went over backwards.

She laughed when he was the one to stand up choking.

They continued splashing around and chasing each other, until finally Eric held up both hands. "Truce?"

Pamela stuck her tongue out at him. "For now—I guess. But when we play Frisbee later, I'm gonna kick your ass!"

He laughed. "Bring it, girlie. I've been practicing, and it's *my* Frisbee."

They were still laughing and teasing each other as they returned to their towels to dry off. Pamela sat down on the blanket again and picked up the sunscreen to apply it to the front side of her, so she could bake on her back for a while. Eric finished off the water in the bottle, then lay on his back next to her.

She looked him over, enjoying the view. She started at his feet, long and well-shaped, like the rest of him. His legs looked almost neon in their whiteness, with curly black hair covering up most of his freckles. That led her eyes up to where the legs disappeared into the silky shorts he was wearing. Still soaking wet, the fabric clung to him, letting her see the outline of what she knew only too well to be a large, well-shaped package, that had never failed to be a source of pleasure for her.

She bit back a sigh as she looked up further. The line of dark hair that extended up to his belly button was mostly covered by the shorts, but she was surprised to see that it had extended itself now to run up between his nipples. He had never had hair on his chest before. Now he had a light fuzzy growth along the center of his chest. His shoulders were still broad, and her toes curled at memories of digging her nails into them while he pounded himself into her as she screamed.

Overcome by a desire to touch him, at any cost, she tried to sound casual. "Hey Eric, want me to rub some sunscreen on you? You're so white I need my sunglasses just to cut down on the glare. I'm afraid you're going to burn in the next five minutes. You might even burst into flames."

He grinned, his eyes still closed. "I'm not a vampire, silly. No flames. I don't even sparkle."

They both laughed.

"Yeah, as if. What kind of self-respecting, blood-sucking-demon sparkles?"

She squirted sunscreen onto her hands then leaned over to rub it all over his chest, stomach and arms. She rubbed up his neck, and realized she was breathing heavily, as she leaned closer to his face. His lips were parted, and she leaned even closer.

He must have felt her breath on his face. He opened his eyes and shook his head slightly. "Don't."

She froze. "Why not?"

"Don't play with me, Mel. It's not fair."

She leaned back with a pout that accentuated her full lips. "Neither is your not letting me touch you. You know why I'm here—why I needed to see you. Why are you fighting me?"

He sighed and sat up, to idly pick up sand and let it run through his fingers. He looked away from her, at the water. "Because you need to decide what you really want, Mel. I'm not going to keep on being your hidden boy-toy. We aren't kids anymore—we're almost thirty years old. I know what I want out of life. I have already achieved some of it. But you're still acting like you're in high school and your parents run your life. You've got a college degree, for God's sake! You own your own business. When are you going to take charge of the personal side of your life, as well as the professional?"

He turned to look at her. As always, she got lost in the infinite depth of blueness in his eyes. "What's it going to be, babe? Door number one, or door number two?"

Her voice was only a whisper. "Which door are you behind?"

He smiled wistfully at her. "Hopefully, the one you pick."

For a long moment they were both lost in each other's gazes, all kinds of things being said in the silence.

Finally she shook her head. "I'm getting kind of hungry, aren't you?"

Eric nodded. "But not for brats yet. How about some ice cream?"

"Aren't the bathrooms up there too?"

"Yeah, right behind the snack bar."

"Then let's go."

They walked, hand in hand, on the wet sand at the water's edge, laughing when it was so deep it slowed them down. They took the time to stop and admire some of the sand sculptures being made by young kids who used buckets, shovels, and bare hands, along with rocks for texture, to create their ephemeral masterpieces.

They both complained about the heat of the hot sand after the cool wet stuff, as they ran up the beach to the snack bar. They perched on a retaining wall while they ate, watching the action on the beach, and commenting on how other people were enjoying themselves.

As usual, there were some who had not realized just how adamant the park rangers were about the *no liquor* rules on the beach. They laughed as some young men who didn't even look old enough to be shaving, tried to argue that beer wasn't really alcohol. "Dude, it's just like soda!" Then the ranger confiscated all their *soda* and drove away.

They ran back towards the water again, strolling at a leisurely pace in the cool, wet sand, back to their towels. They tossed the Frisbee around for a while, without keeping any real score. They just wanted to work off their ice cream. Then once they were out of breath, they lay down, both enjoying the feeling of lying next to each other, even if fully clothed, in public.

When boredom began to set in, Eric challenged Pamela to run up the dunes. They chased each other up, taking turns being in the lead. They raced back down again, to collapse in exhausted heaps when they got to the bottom. Then they did it again. Since they had each won once, they decided that it was best two-of-three and raced up and down one last time.

"You won that last time, I think. Of course, I'm not sure if you cheated or not." Eric's grin let her know he was teasing.

Pamela pulled a pose, with her hands on her hips. "Oh? Is that so, white boy? Maybe you're just a patronizing honkie who's afraid of admitting that a Black woman beat you in a fair race."

They continued to tease each other all the way back to their towels.

When the intense heat of the early afternoon was wearing off, Eric suggested it was time for them to get the coals going and heat up the brats. They collected all their stuff and headed back to the car. They drove to a picnic area that was semi-secluded, and once the coals were going, snuck into the woods to enjoy a couple of beers while they reminisced about when they met for the first time, at that very same park.

Dinner was casual and conversation was light, as they enjoyed each other's company and the time they were spending together. By mutual consent they decided they had had enough of the beach, so after they were done with dinner, they headed back to Eric's cabin.

Their timing was right. They got back to the cabin in enough time to unload all their stuff from the car and put it away, before they headed out to the fire pit to sit on the chairs. They toasted to another gorgeous sunset, with another couple of beers. Afterwards they both sighed with pleasure.

"We need to wash off the sand. Do you want the first shower?" Eric nodded towards the cabin.

Pamela shook her head. "No. I'm gonna sit here for a few more minutes, okay? Go ahead. Just leave me some hot water."

He headed back up the path to the porch.

Once he was gone, Pamela slouched down in her chair to brood. *Now what? Will he start another campfire, to avoid being alone with me in the cabin? Is he waiting for me to make the first move?* She shook her head in consternation. *This isn't easy anymore, like it's always been between us, Eric. I don't know what to do around you now — how to act. It's like we are still old friends, but there's this wall between us, and I don't know how to get through it to reach you.*

She spent a few minutes closing her eyes and concentrating on what she wanted to do to him, what parts of him she particularly wanted to reach for and touch, and how. She felt her toes curling in the sand, and her breathing speeding up. *Damn it, Eric. You have always had this kind of effect on me. And you used to tell me you felt the same way. Do you still?*

She sighed heavily, as she drained the last of her beer, swatting at a persistent mosquito. *Guess it's probably time for my shower now.* She rose and headed up the short path to the porch.

Once in the cabin, she listened hard, but didn't hear the shower running anymore. She peeked into the master bedroom and her heart skipped a beat as she caught a glimpse of Eric's naked butt as he climbed into bed.

He reached for his book, then looked up to see her watching him. He smiled at the look on her face. "I left you some hot water. Some—but not much. Should be enough, at least until you get started trying to rinse the sand out of your hair."

Pamela stuck her tongue out at him. "Thanks, *baldy*. There was a time when you had longer hair than me, you know."

He nodded. "I remember. But those days are long gone, Mel. I'm not a kid anymore. I can't keep trying to look like one."

She had no response, so she went down the hall to take her turn in the shower. She stretched luxuriously as the warmth of the water soothed her skin, itchy and prickly from being covered with sand most of the day. She washed her hair last. As Eric had predicted, she felt the temperature of the water begin to cool as she rinsed out the conditioner. That made her cut short her enjoyment of the shower. A few minutes later she was toweling herself off. She made a face at herself in the bathroom mirror as she began to work the knots out of her hair.

Her mind was racing with imagining how being with Eric would feel again. She was remembering so many moments they had shared, having the best sex of her life. When she was finally ready to exit the bathroom, she was determined to do her best to seduce the man in the master bedroom. She walked out of the bathroom with the towel wrapped around her like a sarong and realized that none of the lights were on anymore.

The only sound was the crashing of the waves on the beach. The only light was the moonlight that spilled in through the windows that faced the water. Taking a deep breath, she headed into the biggest bedroom, afraid of being rejected, yet desperate to touch the man in the bed.

Chapter Ten

Eric was lying on his side, facing the large picture window on the back wall, that faced the beach. He had not closed the blinds, so the moonlight was streaming in, giving an eerie illumination to the room.

Pamela was unsure what to do. *If I ask his permission, he may tell me to go sleep in the bunk bed again. Better to just not ask.* Trying hard not to have her breathing heard by him, she quickly padded barefoot over to the opposite side of the bed. She dropped the towel on the floor and lifted the sheet to slide into bed next to him. She scootched her way over to him and plastered her body to his back. She mashed her breasts against him, curving her legs against his, feeling his butt cheeks tighten as she wrapped her left arm around the front of him, to gently stroke down his chest. She moved her hand up and down, from his wide shoulders, to his bellybutton. As she did, she traced a path with her lips between his shoulder blades, and inhaled deeply, enjoying the scent of the man.

She sighed deeply, not caring anymore that he heard her. Her hand began to stroke lower on his abdomen, and she pushed past his eager cock that reared up in excitement at her touch, to grasp it at the root, her fingers wrapped in the curly hair that covered his ball sac.

With a heavy groan, he turned to face her, propping himself up on his elbow. He wrapped his other hand in her hair and held her face still, as he looked deeply into her eyes, shining in the moonlight that shone over his shoulder. Slowly he leaned his head down and his lips brushed gently against hers. One light kiss, then another. Their passion ignited like a wildfire. He crushed her lips with his, probing her open mouth with his tongue, his hands suddenly stroking all over her body, renewing their familiarity with her every part.

She moaned as he palmed each breast in turn, the nipples already hard as rocks, attempting to poke holes in his hands. He lowered his head to lick and suck at first one, then the other. As he did so, he twisted the other one between his thumb and his forefinger, pulling on it, then rubbing it, doing the same thing with his fingers that he was doing with his mouth.

Pamela moaned again, her body responding to his familiar touch with an ache that she hadn't been able to satisfy for years. Her hips moved back and forth on the bed, her pelvis thrust up in frustration, as he continued to focus all his attention on her sensitive breasts. He was licking at the skin all over them, kneading their ample flesh, burying his head in-between them, only to push them together and suck both nipples into his mouth at the same time.

While he was performing exquisite torture on her with his mouth, his one hand moved downward to stroke her thighs open, as he traced up and down the insides of her upper legs, tickling at the creases at the top of them, making her cells vibrate with the sensations he was creating in her body.

She had reached up to grip the bars on the headboard with both hands, holding on with such force that she was afraid she would pull them off. Now she peeled her fingers off and reached both hands down to stroke along the sides of his body to find him more than ready. With one hand she traced a path along the curve at the small of his back, making his hips involuntarily jerk forward. With the other she stroked his shaft, grown huge and engorged.

He moved closer to her, his one thigh already between her legs, urging them open. She pushed her hips forward to welcome him.

Abruptly he stopped and searched her eyes in the moonlight. "Condom?" His voice was only a throaty growl, not the timber of his usual low tenor.

She shook her head, licking her lips to allow for her to speak with an unsteady voice. "Pill."

"Yes!" His grin was triumphant, as he pushed his hips forward, burying himself up to the balls in her welcoming wet heat.

She gasped with the force of his entry. Almost immediately she felt herself spiral off into an orgasm that took her breath away. She groaned as she felt herself clench around him, as he pounded into her. Each time he pulled back she pushed forward, only to have him shove himself back into her with a force that moved her further towards the headboard each time, until she felt her head pressing against it, with a pillow the only barrier protecting her from the bars.

Each time he pushed into her, she felt another wave of orgasms wash over her, leaving her gasping for breath as if she were drowning. When Eric stopped pulling out of her completely, and his thrusts grew shallower, she knew what to do from years of experience with his body. She concentrated on tightening every muscle in her body simultaneously, tilting her pelvis forward to allow him maximum entrance into her slick core.

His pelvic bone rubbed at her clit as he ground himself against her, and she felt him batter at her cervix. The sensations combined to send her over the edge again, only this time Eric came with her. With a howl he pushed forward one last time, and she felt him spasm inside of her, twitching at every squeeze of her inner muscles, as she rode the tidal waves of her own orgasms, intensified by his.

She opened her eyes to see him suspended above her, his face in a grimace of pleasure, the cords on the sides of his neck straining, the muscles of his arms knotted with the effort he must be putting forth to keep himself upright. Suddenly he collapsed forward onto her, a boneless heap of satisfied man, oblivious to the *whoosh* of air he pushed out of her as he crushed her beneath him.

His face was buried in the pillow next to her head. They lay like that for a long time, their breathing only gradually slowing down to return to independent patterns. When Pamela could move her arms again, she gently stroked his back, running the tips of her fingers down to the curve under his buttocks to give a gentle squeeze, then back up to his broad shoulders, enjoying the feel of his weight on her, holding her down.

It was difficult, but she drew in a long breath, feeling a weight being released from the pit of her stomach. *He still loves me!* She had tears welling in her eyes and tried to stop them, but they ran backwards down the sides of her face. Her breath came in short gasps, as the tension she had been under for days released itself abruptly.

Eric rolled off to one side of her, resting his head on his hand atop his bent arm. He used the fingers on his other hand to trace the line of her tears down the sides of her face.

She tried not to meet his gaze because she was embarrassed.

He gently, but insistently turned her head back, to look deeply into her eyes, watching her as she sobbed. Feeling the need to explain, she sniffed in staggered breaths. When she spoke her voice sounded small and vulnerable, even to her. "I was afraid that you didn't love me anymore. When you wouldn't touch me, I was so afraid that I'd lost you. Then what would I do?"

His smile was soft, the look in his eyes unmistakable, even in the dim moonlight. He shook his head at her. He spoke in a low, quiet voice, while caressing the side of her face. "Before he died, my dad warned me not to ever fall in love so deeply, that I wouldn't want to live without that woman. He tried to make me promise him, but I couldn't. I didn't have the heart to tell him that it was already too late. That a caramel-colored girl with big brown eyes already owned my soul, and that I would never be whole without her. That all I was living was a half-life, and that I had no pride when it came to her. I need you like I need to breathe, Mel."

With a small cry, she reached her arms up to pull him back down to her. They spent the rest of the night making love, pleasuring each other as only they knew how to do, rejoicing in how right it felt to move together again. They finally fell asleep from exhaustion, wrapped in each other's arms, when the first glimmers of daylight were already appearing over the horizon.

Pamela opened her eyes and realized she was still smiling from the night before. She stretched luxuriously before reaching for her lover. The sheets were cold on his side of the bed, and he wasn't there. More fully awake and now curious, she threw off the sheet and made a brief stop in the bathroom. After splashing some water on her face, she listened for some noise to indicate where Eric was, before going in search of her man.

She wandered naked through the house, then found him sitting on the back porch sipping coffee. His hair was still wet, which explained the number of wet towels in the bathroom. He was dressed in running shorts and a sleeveless tee shirt, and his shoes were in front of him, his socks next to his feet on the coffee table. He was sipping coffee while gazing at the beach. He looked up at her expectantly.

Trying for a casual tone, Pamela cleared her throat. "Dressed already? And here I was, hoping for a reprise of last night to get my day off to a great start."

Eric smiled at her, his eyes sweeping over her, making it obvious he was enjoying the look of her nakedness. He answered her in the same light teasing tone she had used. "Are you serious, woman? I didn't think I was capable of coming that many times in one night anymore! I might be able to *get it up* in the near future, but I'm sure it will take a lot longer before I would be able to come again. You plum wore me out, little lady. I tip my hat to you."

She smiled mischievously back at him. "Are you sure? I could give it the *old college try*, you know."

He made a face at her. "I really don't want to think about what you were doing when you were away at college."

She sat down to face him, and drank in the sight of his strong arms, his broad shoulders, and his long legs stretching out in front of him. "Why? I never got what I wanted there. I always had to come back to you for that."

He sighed heavily, as he bent down to pull his socks on, then to slide his feet into his shoes and tie them up. "You still haven't made your choice yet, Mel. What's between us is the same as it's always been. But I can't go on like this—seeing you only when you need to run to me for understanding. You have to either decide to stay with me and damn the consequences—or you have to cut me loose, and never come back. It's your choice."

She felt her heart begin to race at the idea of not seeing him anymore. The ache that gnawed at the pit of her stomach was too frighteningly familiar. She leaned forward urgently. "Why do I have to choose?"

He raised his eyebrows to glare at her. "Haven't you been listening? Because you're the one who keeps running away from me. I'm where I've always been. You know where to find me, when you do decide."

He stood up decisively. "For now, I'm going for a long run on the beach, and I don't want you to be here when I get back.

There's some coffee left, and you can always make more for the ride, if you want. There's a couple of thawed bagels on the counter, with some frozen fruit in a bowl in the fridge. You know you can help yourself to anything that you find. But today is Monday. I have to head in to work by about two in the afternoon at the latest. So I'll be leaving right after I get back from my run. And you have to get that car back to O'Hare."

She tried not to look as bereft as she felt. "So this is *good-bye* then?"

His eyes swept across her naked body, then burned into hers, as he spoke urgently, yet passionately. "That's up to you, Mel. You know where to find me. But at least do me the courtesy of letting me know if you decide to follow your parents' plan for your life. My cell phone is on the counter in the kitchen, and I wrote the number down for you. Call me when you've made up your mind."

He walked by her and headed out the door. She watched as he strode quickly down to the fire ring to stretch. Then he began an easy lope along the beach. She watched until she couldn't see him anymore, once he ran past a large cabin that jutted out almost into the water.

With a long sigh, Pamela headed back into the bathroom to take a quick shower. She pulled on the tee shirt and jeans that she had put on when she left her *real life* behind, out of desperation. Then she made her way into the kitchen to eat something, and to make another pot of coffee.

While she sat and ate, she decided to do what her mother had taught her to do years ago, when she had difficult decisions to make. She found a piece of blank computer paper, and she drew a line down the middle of it, labeling one side *Donald*, and the other side *Eric*. Under each name she made another two columns, labeled *Good* and *Bad*. She wrote for a long time, sometimes staring off into space, sometimes chewing on the pencil thoughtfully, as she tried to put her choices onto paper.

Sometime later, she reread what she had written yet again. *I'll leave this here. He needs to see this. Maybe this will let him know what I've decided.*

With that, she packed up her few belongings and threw them into the back seat of the rental car. With a last long look off into the horizon, hoping to see some sign of Eric returning to kiss her goodbye, she sighed again, before pulling out of the driveway to head back to the reality of her life. She was not looking forward to facing the music caused by her rash decisions of a few days ago. But she was determined that this time she would be strong enough to do what she had to do.

Chapter Eleven

For once in her life, Pamela did not exceed the speed limit as she drove from her parents' condo to the apartment that she shared with Donald. She was not looking forward to talking to him, but she had to make arrangements to get her belongings out. Besides, her mother was right. She did owe him the courtesy of an explanation, and the chance to try to change her mind.

She smiled as she shook her head slowly. *Not that that is possible anymore. Why on earth would I agree to spend the rest of my life with someone for whom I am only second, or maybe third in importance? I have spent years trying to find someone that I really matter to. In reality, I think I always knew I would make this choice, sooner or later. I guess I'm finally strong enough to admit it and deal with the consequences.*

Her mind replayed the last twenty-four hours, and she was relieved that it was now in the past. It had been as bad as she was afraid of — no, she corrected herself, it was worse.

After returning the rental car, she had taken the el into the city and gotten off at the stop closest to her parents' condo. Then she had grabbed a cab with the little money she had left, and she had appeared in the lobby of their building in clothes that she had worn for days, looking sun-burned and disheveled, and not a little bit apologetic.

She told the security guard that she was here to see her parents. He asked her who her parents were, without looking up. When she said their names, he looked up quickly.

"Hey, aren't you *the runaway bride* lady?"

She nodded wearily. "Uh huh."

She tried to ignore his furtively taking out his cell phone to snap a quick picture while she was dialing her parents on the house security phone.

"Hello," her dad said formally into the phone when he picked it up.

"Hi Dad, can I come up to see you?"

His tone changed entirely, to one of surprise and delighted joy. "Pamela? Are you all right? Honey, it's Pamela!"

She smiled at his tone. "Yes, Dad. I'm fine. I'm in the lobby. Can I come up?"

"Of course you can!"

He punched the buttons on his console in the condo to talk to the security guard, speaking so loudly that she could hear every word. "Send my daughter up immediately."

"Yes, sir."

Pamela walked slowly over to the elevator with heavy feet. She was so not looking forward to this. But she had to explain to her parents what had happened. She owed them that much. She sighed as the elevator door slid closed and whisked her up to the twenty-fifth floor condo, with its panoramic view of the skyline and the beautiful blue jewel of Lake Michigan beyond it.

As the elevator door opened on their floor, her parents' door was thrown open and her father appeared in the doorway, looking expectantly at the elevator. He ran down the hall to pull her into his arms. "Pamela! Sweetheart! We've been so worried about you! You didn't call—not one word to let us know you were all right."

He crushed her into one of his bear hugs, and for a moment she allowed his love to just wash over her, reminding her of all the homecomings in her past, when he had always been thrilled to have her back home. How she had longed for that love to be always in her life—how unfortunately it never took long before everything was back to *normal,* and she would be driven to run away again, just to force him to admit to her how much he loved her.

"I love you too, Dad," she said.

Finally he let her go and kept only his arm around her shoulders, as they walked back to the open condo door.

"Where's Mom?"

"At the kitchen table, crying."

Her dad gave her a stern look. "You've run away before, but never for so long. Three whole days! Your mother has been worried sick over you. You had better have a good explanation for your behavior, young lady."

Pamela rolled her eyes. It had taken even less time than usual for him to go from being relieved, loving father, to stern disciplinarian, and protector of her mother.

Her mother was indeed sitting at the table and was too overcome to even get up when she got into the room. Pamela walked over to her mother to stand in front of her.

"I'm sorry for worrying you like this, Mom."

Her mother reached out her arms and Pamela hugged her, both crying as her mother's sobs shook her slender shoulders.

After the storm of emotion was done, her father brought in a pot of coffee, and the second-degree began, along with the accusations.

While she was explaining, Pamela tried not to think that her mother was even more concerned about what Donald was going to think about her reappearance. But her mom seemed determined to insert his name into the discussion at every opportunity. Finally Pamela got irritated enough to object.

"Honestly, Mom, he's not the main concern here. I'm sorry I worried you and Dad, but I really needed to get away for a little while, to think more clearly about everything. And I have made some decisions. First of all, I'm not going to marry Donald."

Her mother frowned. "Well, of course he's going to be up-set with you, but I'm sure once you explain things to him, he'll see that you are all back to normal, and the wedding can be re-scheduled. Maybe not as big of an event, but still—"

Pamela shook her head firmly. "No, Mom. I'm *never* going to marry him. He's all wrong for me. I see that now. I was never as much in love with him as you wanted me to be. But his letting me know just where I ranked in importance in his life was the final straw. It forced me to see him for the self-absorbed upwardly mobile jerk that he is. So he and I are through. I'll be going to see him soon to tell him that, and to get all of my things out of the apartment."

Her mother was shocked, and even her father was sur-prised. They cajoled her, trying to pry out of her just where she had been for the past few days, since she left the hotel that Donald and her dad had tracked her to. She told them only that she had taken a few days off to give some serious thought to what she really wanted out of her life. They were not satis-fied, but finally gave up. They ordered some Thai food to be delivered for dinner, and Pamela excused herself to go to the guest room to pick some clean clothes out of what she had left there the last time she was visiting. She took a shower and changed.

They had left her cell phone in the guest room, and the first thing she did once she was out of the shower and dressed, was to program Eric's number into it. Then she dialed him.

"Hi, if you're calling Eric Taylor, leave a message. I'll get back to you when I can."

She made a face at the phone. She had been thrilled to hear his voice, as if just hearing him gave her a boost in her strength. Her parents were a formidable force when they united, and right now they were determined to uncover what-ever she was hiding from them.

"Hi Eric, it's me. I'm at my parents' place now. They are

really pissed at me, so it's kind of hard to tell them about us. I don't think they're ready yet. I'll call you when I can." She smiled as she put the phone down. Then she got up, straightened her shoulders, and strode back into the lion's den.

Her mother was glaring at her, and even her father looked shocked.

"Eric? That bum you used to date in high school? That—that mechanic? The grease monkey?"

Pamela felt her heart start to race. "What were you guys doing? Listening in on what I was doing? Spying on me? I'm almost thirty years old, damn it! Don't I get to have a private life?"

Her mother spat out her disgust. "That jerk wasn't good enough for you when you were teenagers. His dad was a drunk, and—"

"His mom was dying. That's why his dad drank. Because he was so devastated by her cancer. You need to learn the facts before you pass judgment."

"I don't care what the reason was. He was a drunk, and that's genetic. I won't have any of my grandchildren born to a father who is a drunk."

"Eric is not a drunk!"

"So you admit that you were with him for the past few days?"

Her dad was glaring at her too, and once again Pamela felt reduced to the status of a small child who had been caught with her hand in the cookie jar. "What if I was? He loves me. He's always loved me. And I love him. I ran to him because he's the one I've always run to when I needed comfort."

"For how long? You mean to tell us you have been seeing him since high school?"

Her father was incredulous. Her mother was working up to a full-fledged temper tantrum.

Pamela nodded.

They took turns telling her what a bum this man was. How wrong he was for her. How her life would be a disaster once she married beneath her station. How guys like him expect to be supported by their women. How he probably had a string of ex-wives, with children by each of them. When she looked guilty at that, they knew they had struck a nerve, and the insults intensified.

Through it all, Pamela tried to keep up a brave front, and said as little as possible. Inwardly she concentrated on the way she felt when Eric held her, and she tried to focus on that. She ignored the opinions of him being expressed by her parents, who had never taken any time to get to know him, because they had dismissed him immediately as being not good enough for their daughter.

Eventually her mother insisted that she call Donald and tell him when she would see him. Her mother pressed for that night, but Pamela pleaded tiredness.

"I'll go talk to him tomorrow, Mom. Honestly, don't you think listening to the two of you is enough torture for one day? I'm tired and I want to get some sleep before I have to face him."

"Yes, I suppose you'll be better able to break his heart and ruin his life after a good night's sleep." Her mother had always been the kind of woman to turn nasty when she didn't get her way.

With a shrug, Pamela called Donald's number. "Hello, Donald?"

Her parents could hear him yelling on the phone. "Pamela? Is that you? Where are you, honey? I'll be right there."

"No. I'm too tired to see you tonight."

"Are you in pain? Are you hurt?"

"No, I'm fine. I'm staying tonight at my parents' condo. I can come by to see you in the morning."

"I'll have brunch here for you, sweetheart. Can you be here

by eleven?"

"Sure. I'll see you then."

"I love you, Pamela. You're my world."

She grimaced. "See you tomorrow, Donald."

Since there wasn't anything else that her parents had to say that Pamela wanted to hear, she pleaded exhaustion and locked herself in the guest bedroom. She could hear her parents talking in the living room for a long time.

She thought about calling her answering service, but realized she didn't need to, since she'd already arranged for a two-week vacation that was supposed to be her honeymoon. After that, since she didn't want her parents to be able to hear her, she went into the attached guest bathroom. She turned on the fan before she dialed Eric's number again. This time he answered on the first ring.

"Hi Eric, it's me."

His voice sounded relieved. "Hi honey. It's good to hear your voice."

Pamela surprised herself by bursting into tears.

"Mel! What's wrong?"

She tried to pull herself together, but only managed a few words in-between sobs. "They hate you."

There was a short silence then a long sigh from Eric. "Did you tell them about us? Is that why?"

Pamela nodded and sniffed into the phone. "Um hmm. They were spying on me and heard me leave you a message."

Eric's voice was gentle as he spoke. "Honey, I found the list you made. I was really amused by it, and by your leaving it where I would find it. At first, I was extremely jealous by your writing, *sometimes good sex* under Donald's name. Then I read the rest of both lists."

Pamela sniffed loudly again. "Did you read the end of it? The last thing I wrote under your name?"

"You mean after *we always make love,* and *makes me feel*

cherished? Do you mean *he would die for me,* and *I would die for him too?"*

Pamela smiled through her tears. "Um-hmm."

Eric's voice was gentle. "Did you mean it, babe?"

Pamela sniffled while she nodded into the phone. "Every word."

Eric let out a long, satisfied sigh. "You have no idea just how long I've been waiting to hear that from you."

"Yes, I think I do."

"Is there anything I can do to help you over the next couple of days? Come and talk to your parents? Challenge your soon-to-be-ex-fiancé to arm-wrestling? I think I could take him, you know. He may make more money than I do, but I work with my hands, and I work out regularly. I learned to fight dirty from my older brother, and I ride a Harley, so I've been in my share of fights in biker bars. Sometimes I even win." He cleared his throat. "On second thought, don't mention any of that to your parents, okay?"

Pamela managed to giggle. "Oh, you could take him all right. He's a big man when he's in rich people company. But he's not a *real man*, like you are."

There was a companionable silence for a few minutes, while Pamela gradually stopped crying and Eric waited for her to speak again.

"I'm going to go see Donald tomorrow for lunch. I'll tell him then that the wedding's off. Then I'll make arrangements to get my stuff out of his apartment. I haven't been living there that long, so there's not a whole lot to move."

"Where will you move it to?"

She paused for a heartbeat. "Well—I suppose I could move it in here, to my parents' guest room. Just until I figure out where I'll be living."

Eric cleared his throat. "Or you could move it here, to my place. It's not a big apartment. It only has one bedroom. But it's a big room. And there's a queen-sized bed in it that needs someone to start sleeping on the other side of it, so the mattress gets worn evenly."

Pamela stopped breathing for a split second, her heart racing. "Why Eric Taylor. Are you asking me to move in with you?"

His smile was audible over the phone. "Uh-huh. That way I can drive you so crazy with wild monkey sex, that you'll forget you ever had any pleasure with any other man. I'll trick you into marrying me somehow, knock you up a few times, and then my life will be complete. You'll never get away from me again. Mwah-hah-hah-hah!"

Pamela giggled. "Oh Eric. You curl my toes. I love you. You know that don't you?"

"You've said that before, Mel. Actions speak louder than words. Until I have you in my arms again, I'll still be worried that somehow the vast conspiracy of your parents and their cohorts will somehow take you away from me again."

Pamela shook her head. "Uh-uh. Never again. I've finally admitted to myself what I've been denying for years. You're the only man I want, and I want to spend the rest of my life with you. If you'll have me."

Eric sighed once again. "I live for that moment, Mel."

"Then I'll see you soon. I'd better get some sleep, since I have a feeling that Donald isn't going to take my news any better than my parents did."

"Okay, honey. You get some rest and be sure to dream of me, like I'll be dreaming of you."

"I will. Oh, and Eric?"

"What?"

"Thanks for waiting for me to make up my mind. If you had pressured me, I might have run away from you too."

"Mel, if there's one thing I've learned over all of these years of loving you, it's that you run away easily, like a spooked racehorse. But you're always worth waiting for. I'll be here, waiting for you."

Pamela sighed with relief tinged with anticipation. "Goodnight, Eric."

"Goodnight, babe. Be strong."

Pamela sat and looked at the phone for a few moments, with a huge smile on her face. *It feels so good to finally admit to myself what I really want in life. I'm so glad I bolted from the church, so I don't have to get a divorce from the wrong man, to be with the right man.* She got up and changed into a nightgown, to go to bed and dream about what her life with Mr. Right was going to be like.

Chapter Twelve

So now here she was, driving to have brunch with the man she had left in the church, running away as if the devils of hell were after her. *And maybe they were,* she mused.

At any rate, she wasn't sure if this was going to be the easier of the two confrontations she had to have, or if Donald was going to be even more trouble than her parents had been. Either way, she was soon to find out.

She let herself into the apartment with her key, to see that the dining room table was set with the formal china, and there were dozens of roses all around the room in vases. There was jazz music playing softly in the background, and an open bottle of Dom Perignon was chilling near the table.

She sniffed appreciatively and realized that since Donald didn't even know how to boil water without getting it all over the stove, he must have hired someone to come in and do some serious cooking before she got there. She listened intently, but heard no conversation, so she figured the cook, or cooks, must be gone. Donald was no doubt in the kitchen waiting for her to appear.

"Hello? Anyone here?"

Donald appeared in the doorway of the kitchen and immediately rushed up to fold her into a big hug.

"Pamela! I'm so relieved! I was so worried about you! Are you all right my love?" He tried to kiss her on the lips.

She turned her head away from him quickly. She spoke to give herself a reason to not kiss him. "Who did all of this cooking? I can smell cinnamon and sausages. What on earth is all of this?"

He smiled at her warmly. "It's just my way of letting you know how much I missed you, and how happy I am that you have come back to me."

She cleared her throat. "Yeah—about that. We have to talk."

He nodded. "Of course we'll talk. But for now, let's eat. You just go sit down at the table and pour yourself some champagne. I'll bring everything in."

Once he had placed all the food dishes on the table, he uncovered one after another. There was cinnamon-glazed french toast, the gourmet sausages that he liked so much from one of the trendier spots nearby that he liked to be seen eating in frequently, and fluffy scrambled eggs with asparagus and feta cheese. There was also a fruit salsa made with mixed chopped berries, and tiny cinnamon crisps to dip into the salsa.

Everything on the table was something that she had particularly enjoyed when they had eaten it in the local restaurants. The look on his face was tenderly expectant, and she was touched by his obvious desire to please her. *A little too late, as always, but sweet none-the-less.*

"Well? What are you waiting for? Ladies first, you know. I can't take anything until you do, and I don't know about you, but I'm starved."

Pamela smiled at him and helped herself to some of all the choices.

He solicitously poured her another glass of champagne.

"Aren't you having any champagne?"

Donald shook his head and indicated his tall glass and a nearby pitcher.

"No, I don't like it as much as you do. I'm having bloody marys instead."

She nodded as she chewed slowly, enjoying all the food with gusto. When she was finally too full to eat anymore, she pushed the plate away, and Donald poured the last of the champagne into her glass.

"I think I might like some coffee," she said. "I'm feeling a real buzz from drinking so early in the day."

"Sure." He poured some coffee for both from the nearby thermal pot.

"Now tell me, Pamela, my love, where were you all of this time, while we were supposed to be on our honeymoon?"

She took a deep breath before she answered him. "I was — um — chilling out somewhere, thinking over what I really want out of life."

He leaned forward. "And? If you want breakfasts like this every day, that can be arranged. Once I make full partner, there's almost no limit as to what we'll be able to afford, you know. I'll even be able to help you expand your little pet place, if you want to."

She made a face at him. "Little pet place? You mean my veterinary practice?"

He nodded. "Yeah, whatever. I mean, of course you'll have to give it up once we start having children. But for now, you can keep it."

She tried to control her anger that seemed to spring up out of nowhere. She took a few deep breaths, which seemed to help a little. "While I was away, I came to a decision, Donald. You are not going to like it, but please respect me enough to listen to what I have to say." She took another deep breath, feeling herself sway in her chair a bit. She took another sip of coffee, to try to sober herself up. "I'm not going to marry you, Donald. I don't love you. I mean, I like you, but you are not the man I want to spend the rest of my life with."

Hi eyebrows rose into his hair, his face reflecting shock.

"It's nothing that you did, it's me. I haven't been happy for a while, but the plans were so huge, and everything was moving along so quickly, that I was too busy to even think about whether or not I wanted to marry you. Which I don't."

He leaned forward. "But Pamela, what about all of our plans? I'm in the running to make partner in the next couple of months, and for that I need a wife."

She shook her head. "It's not going to be me, Donald. But don't worry. You're a good-looking guy—good in bed too. It shouldn't be that hard for you to find someone else as upwardly mobile as yourself, to be willing to play the *wifey* role for you." She rolled her eyes. "How could you think I was going to be happy playing the same role that I've watched my mom doing my whole life? God, I hate having to play all of those kiss-ass suck-up games with people I don't like! When I was younger, they would make me come out and perform for the partners and their wives—like I was some kind of trained monkey. I would play the piano for them, and they'd all clap politely. But it was excruciating for me. I hated it then. I would hate it even more now."

Donald narrowed his eyes at her. "Why didn't you tell me all of this earlier? Like when we were making our wedding plans?"

"I tried to! But you wouldn't listen. You're just like my mom. You pretend to hear what I'm saying, but then you follow up with telling me how I should act, how I should feel, and not giving me a choice. I'm a grown up. I'm tired of people telling me how I need to be. I want to make my own choices."

Pamela was beginning to wonder if the air conditioning was broken in the apartment. She could feel rivulets of sweat running down her back, and she felt flushed. Her hand shook as she reached for the coffee cup. She took a quick sip then set it back down hurriedly, hoping that Donald didn't notice.

He was too angry to notice anything. "What the fuck are you telling me? That all of a sudden you are not in love with me anymore, and that you don't want to be a part of my life?

Is there something you're not telling me about your weekend? Like maybe, where you slept? Or with whom?"

Pamela tried not to look guilty but was finding it increasingly difficult to disguise her emotions, while her body appeared to be slipping out from under her control. She was trying not to panic, but the more she tried not to, the more she could feel her heart beginning to race in her chest.

"What do you mean?" Even her tongue was beginning to lump in her mouth, making speech increasingly difficult.

"Isn't it true that you were with another guy? Some lowlife you dated back in high school? The kind of guy who fixes my car? What, were you enjoying slumming it with a blue-collar biker? Am I too much of a gentleman for you? Is that it? Do you want a man who grunts and scratches and forces himself on you? Do you want to be dominated? Because that's easy to arrange."

She shook her head, but to her horror, found it made her feel dizzy. She tried to glare at Donald, but he was beginning to look fuzzy. Vaguely she remembered having felt like this before. *When was that? Oh yeah — back in college. Shareena brought those drugs to a party at my house. All us girls got so wasted we ended up throwing all of the guys out. We sat around drinking and talking all night.*

"Donald," she panted. "Did you — ?"

His grin was evil and triumphant. "I wondered when you'd notice. I didn't want to over-do it and have you pass out with your face in your eggs."

"You — you drugged me?"

He nodded, looking smug. "Yup. Your mom called me last night and told me all about your plans to dump me for some low-class biker. Did you honestly think it was going to be that easy to get away from me? After all I've invested in you?"

She was finding it increasingly difficult to concentrate, but he kept talking, pacing around the room as he spoke.

"The partnership is only going to be offered to one lawyer,

Pamela. Word is that the senior partners are looking to add some diversity to the firm. That's the one thing I can't even fake. I can't be anything other than the blond white boy that I am. But with you as my wife, with pictures of little bi-racial kids on my desk? I'll be the next best thing they've got. My place will be guaranteed secure for the next twenty years. That's why I can't marry anyone else, sweetie. It's got to be you. Fortunately your mom agrees with me."

He stopped to stand in front of her, glaring at her. It made her dizzy to look up at him. "When Maribel called and told me it was some other guy, first I got angry. Then I asked her some questions. Seems you've been stringing this guy along for years. So I figured maybe he finally wanted you to make a choice between him and me. He's probably waiting to hear from you. So my plan is to keep you here as long as it takes for him to lose interest."

He grabbed her shoulders and pulled her up out of the chair. When she wobbled, he put one arm around her back and held her up. He guided her into walking the short distance down the hall and into the bedroom. "And while I've got you in such an agreeable mood, I'm going to have some fun. You like it rough with a biker? Fine. I can do rough. In fact, I've got a secret to tell you, Pamela. I like it rough. Really rough. In fact, I've been holding back all of this time, waiting until we were married, when you wouldn't be able to object anymore. I'm going to really enjoy this. A little bit of tying you up, slapping you around. I don't know if you'll like it as much as I will, but then, you won't remember it anyway, so who gives a shit?" He chuckled evilly as he pushed her onto the bed and started to undress her.

She tried to resist him, but her limbs were unresponsive, and her brain was fogging over. She made a feeble attempt to protest. "But that's rape!"

He chuckled again. "Rape? When you're my fiancée and

everyone in the Chicago area knows that from seeing you make a fool of me, by running away on TV? When you let yourself in with your own key, because you live here? When your own mother tipped me off about the other guy, and begged me to do *anything it takes* to stop you from ruining your life? She said you need to marry me. Who do you think is going to believe you, after you've been acting so irrationally?"

He tugged on her pants, taking the panties off along with them. "Besides," he smirked, "It's only rape if you say *no*, try to fight me off, and remember what happened the next day. You won't—lucky for me!"

With an evil laugh he pushed her over onto her stomach and slapped her hard across the butt. She moaned, but was unable to do anything about her nakedness, and his taunts. He slapped her ass a few more times. "Is this rough enough for you? I hope not, because I'm just getting started."

She felt the bed move as he got onto it behind her. He lifted her up to slide a pillow under her belly. She made a last feeble attempt to resist, but to her horror she discovered that her mouth wouldn't let sounds come out anymore. Her last conscious thought was, *No!* Then everything went black.

Chapter Thirteen

Pamela was drowning. She felt the water trickle down the back of her throat, felt it entering her lungs. She reared up choking, trying to fight it, trying to get to the surface.

"Hey, you crazy bitch! Watch it! You've got a wicked right cross there. Don't you dare hit me again."

She shook her head. "What's going on?"

"I just thought you'd be thirsty after all you drank yesterday. So I was giving you some water."

"Bullshit! You asshole! You're drugging me again!" She flailed with her arms, but found they still weren't fully under her control.

Donald was able to easily evade her by taking a step backwards. He stood still and watched her, his arms folded across his chest. "Yes I am. I told you I'm keeping you here until you come to your senses."

"How can I come to them if you keep drugging me?"

He smirked. "Well okay, I want you to come around to agreeing with me. Until you do, you're going to be naked and in my bed. I'll get to have my fun with you while you are passed out, then we can have these nice little chats when you wake up, before the drugs kick in again."

Pamela felt herself starting to drift off again and tried hard to fight it. "You can't keep me here forever. Nothing you can do to me is going to make me agree to stay with you."

Donald shook his head, then pulled a chair over and sat backwards on it, leaning over the back of the chair as he spoke. "I've been thinking about that. The way I see it, worst case scenario is you continue to refuse. Eventually I will have to let you out of here, if only because I will have to go to court, so I won't be here to keep you confined. Even if I tied you to the bed, you might still be able to scream loudly enough to draw attention to yourself. Before that happens, I'll give you a massive dose, drag you out to Las Vegas, and we'll have a quickie wedding that only requires you to mumble when we say our vows. By that time, I'll have been fucking you multiple times a day without you taking your birth control pills. You left them here, remember? So you haven't had them for what, four days now? If I'm lucky, you'll be pregnant by the time I get a ring on your finger. And you are so against abortion that you wouldn't even consider that option. So then you'll be mine for a long time."

She shook her head groggily, speaking with great effort. "I'd be — happy — to abort — your — evil spawn."

His grin was pure evil. "We'll see. Now you look about ready for another reminder of what you've been missing while you were gone. And we're in luck. Here's me with another stiffie, just for you."

She moaned before blacking out again.

The sound is familiar. An alarm clock? A kitchen timer? A phone? Yes. A cell phone! My cell phone! She tried to open her eyes, but found they were not responding to her commands.

Donald spoke from very close to her. "Hello? Oh, hi Maribel. Pamela? Uh — she's asleep right now."

He chuckled in a low, sexy manner. "Well, yes, as a matter of fact, we were up really late last night, celebrating being back together again. You know what that's like."

He listened then chuckled again. "Oh, you don't have to worry about us anymore. Pamela has come to her senses once and for all. In fact, we may just do something rash and crazy and fly out for a quickie wedding out in Vegas."

He was quiet for a moment. "Yes, I agree. The stress of the big wedding is probably what made her run away and think she wasn't happy with me. I think if we elope, she'll be a whole lot happier. And we may just have some good news for you when we get back."

He was quiet again. "Well, the only hint I can give you is that she's not taking her pills anymore."

He listened then responded again. "No, nothing yet. But it's really too soon to tell. I promise, you'll be the first to know."

"Damn!" He swore softly under his breath. "Listen, I hate to cut you off and all, but my cell phone is ringing out in the living room. I'm expecting an urgent call from one of the big guys. If it's him, I'll have to jump onto the computer and do some work while Pamela catches up on her beauty sleep. So I'll have to talk to you again really soon, okay?" He clicked the phone off and threw it onto the desk by the door, on his way out to the living room.

Pamela heard him answer the phone out there, then his voice trailed away as he walked towards his office at the other end of the apartment. Her brain was fighting to work, trying to tell her something. *Donald left my phone in the room. He thinks I'm still asleep. But I'm not. I'm in his apartment. All I have to do is walk over to the desk and pick up the phone. Then I can call for help.*

It took a few attempts, but she was finally able to push herself up to a seated position, with her feet on the floor. She panted from her exertions. Wearily she looked across the room at the desk. *It's so far away! I'll never be able to make it!* She gave herself a mental slap upside the head. *No! I can do this! I have to do this. I can't let him keep doing things to me — things that I can't even remember. I've got to get away from him.*

With great effort, she pushed herself to a standing position. Immediately the room started to spin as she swayed, trying to stay upright. *Just a few steps. Not very far at all. Just a few more steps. I'm almost there. I can almost touch the phone — got it!*

Totally worn out, she collapsed when her knees buckled and gave way underneath her. She lay on the floor panting, as she tried to fight the fog in her brain. *Who can I call? Who will believe me?* She was momentarily overcome with panic. She had the phone in her hand, but even the police wouldn't believe her. Who could she call? *Eric!*

She blinked a few times to clear her vision enough for her to be able to focus on the names on her phone, as she scrolled through them. When she saw *Eric*, she pushed the green button.

It seemed to take forever while the phone rang once — twice — *Please don't let it go to voice mail — please don't let it go to —*

"Hello?"

She licked her lips and tried to speak, but only a croak came out.

"Hello? Who is this? Is this some kind of joke?"

"Eric!"

"Mel? Is that you? You sound awful. Where are you? You haven't called me, and you didn't answer your phone."

"He's drugging me —"

"What?"

"He's drugging me — can't talk —"

"Mel, concentrate. Where are you?"

"The apartment. He's been — doing things to me —"

"Mel, listen to me. I'll kill him after I get you away from him. But you need to tell me, where is the apartment?"

"Please help me —" Despite her best efforts to stay awake, Pamela blacked out again.

CHAPTER FOURTEEN

Eric gnashed his teeth as his mind raced. He had no idea where the asshole's apartment was. He didn't even know the asshole's name. If he could go on-line, he could probably find it in a news story from over the weekend. But guys like that had unlisted, unpublished numbers and addresses. So that was a dead end.

He didn't have a number for Mel's parents either. They weren't in the townhouse she had grown up in anymore. They were in a condo in the city. Probably also unlisted and unpublished. He gnashed his teeth so hard his jaw ached. All he did know was that her father's name was Joseph Wilson, and he was a senior partner in a big law firm downtown. So his name must be listed on the title of the law firm, right?

Eric strode purposefully out to the office in the front of the shop, where Marco, as usual, had the TV on and was watching the news.

"Hey Marco, can I use the computer for a minute?"

Marco looked up. "Yeah sure, Eric. Why? You got something you want to look up for one of the cars?"

Eric shook his head while he navigated into a search engine and started to look for law firms in Chicago with Joseph Wilson as one of the names. "Nah, it's personal. I'm gonna need a little bit of time off too. I've got something I gotta do right now."

Marco raised one eyebrow. "Okay. Just be back in time to get the Sullivan car done before that prick tries to ream me a new one, like he did the last time."

"He's coming tomorrow afternoon, right?"

Marco nodded.

"No problem."

Eric studied the screen intently. "Found it!"

Marco didn't even look up from the TV as Eric wrote quickly on a sticky note.

"Got what you need?"

"Yeah. Bye."

Eric strode quickly out to his Harley, fired up the engine, and roared off in a cloud of black smoke and noise.

Joseph Wilson was in a meeting with a junior partner. They were discussing just how to handle a most sensitive case, one that he had put his neck on the line to have assigned to the young woman he was talking to. But then, there were so few Black lawyers, particularly female ones, that he felt an obligation to do all that he could to help her further her career.

She was in the middle of a long, involved explanation as to exactly how she was handling the particulars, when there was a knock on the door.

They both looked at the door as his secretary walked in apologetically. "Sir, there's a young man in the lobby who is asking for you."

"Sylvia, I told you I wasn't going to take any phone calls. That means no interruptions. And certainly no meetings."

"But sir, he says it's very important. In fact, he said *urgent*. He said it's about your daughter."

Joseph sighed deeply. "Did he say *what* about her?"

The secretary shook her head. "No sir. But isn't her name Pamela? He called her Mel."

Joseph stood up wearily. "I think I'll have to speak to this young man, Charlotte. I'll be right back."

She smiled at him and nodded. "That will give me time to work on some of your suggestions."

He nodded with a tight smile and followed his secretary out the door.

When Joseph walked into the lobby, he wasn't sure what he expected to see. The man who stood up and walked quickly over to him was certainly not the scrawny, long-haired teenager he remembered. This young man was tall, well-built, and had short black hair with blond streaks in the front. He was wearing worn jeans and a tee shirt, with a black leather jacket. He still looked like every father's worst nightmare.

"Eric, I presume?"

Eric nodded. "Mr. Wilson, I would never have bothered you at work. But this is really urgent." He stopped, looking around at the few people sitting in the lobby, and the secretaries who had turned to watch them. "Is there somewhere we can go to talk in private?"

"Young man, I'm very busy. Whatever you have to say can't take that long."

"You need to hear what I have to tell you. Can't you for once, put Mel first instead of last, in your priorities?"

Joseph took a deep calming breath, as he felt his fist curl to punch this biker punk for his rude insinuation. "This way," he said through clenched teeth, leading the younger man down a hall and into his corner office. He sat down behind his massive desk and was proud for an instant of the understated opulence of his surroundings. His triumph was short-lived, as he realized that the young man hadn't even glanced around, but was pacing back and forth in front of the chair he had waved at for him to sit in. "So what is this all about?"

"Sir, all I need from you is the address of the apartment that Mel has been living in with that guy."

"What for? And stop that pacing, boy. Sit down!"

Eric strode over to perch on the very edge of the chair. "I just got a call from Mel, sir. She sounded higher than I've ever heard her. We smoked some weed when we were younger—but she's never been as wasted as she sounded on the phone."

"So?"

"She told me that he's drugging her. She said that he's keeping her prisoner in his apartment. She asked me to help her." He leaned ever further forward, twisting his hands in desperation or supplication. "That's why I need your help. I don't know where the apartment is."

Joseph tried for nonchalance, but even to his ears, his laugh sounded uneasy. "You must be joking. Donald is a respected attorney at a very large, very important firm right around the corner from here. What on earth makes you think I'm going to believe some cock-a-mamie story like this? You come barging into my office, with some unbelievable story about my daughter calling you—exactly why? If she is in trouble, wouldn't she call her father first? Or the police? Why you?"

Eric jumped up to begin pacing again. "I don't know why she called me. Except that she knows she can count on me. Please, sir, just give me the address." Eric looked beseechingly at the older man.

Joseph sat silently regarding him with obvious suspicion.

Finally Eric spoke again, taking deep breaths, trying to sound more rational. "Look, sir. Just give me the address. I promise, if I get there and it's just some kind of joke, I'll never bother you ever again."

Joseph leaned backward in his chair, his elbows on the armrests, his fingers tapping together, as he considered his words carefully. "Let's just presume for a moment that I even partially believe you, which I really don't. To my mind, the best way for you to prove you are not lying, or for me to see that you are, is if I come with you. Since I know where the apartment is, you will follow me there."

Eric walked quickly over to the door. "Fine, sir. Let's get going right now."

Joseph regarded him thoughtfully. "You said that if you're wrong, I won't see you again?"

Eric nodded. "Never darken your door again. Let's get going."

Joseph sighed heavily before leaning over to tap at his console. "Sylvia? I'm stepping out for a short time. Tell Charlotte I'll meet with her later today to finish our discussion." He rose from his chair. "I'm driving a black Benz. I presume you are in the parking garage?"

Eric nodded. "I'm parked right by the exit, in one of the motorcycle spaces. I'll watch for you and follow you."

Joseph nodded.

Chapter Fifteen

The traffic was the usual glut of impatient drivers filled with road rage. It took about twenty minutes for them to pull up to the building that had a parking garage on the third floor. Eric followed Joseph to the spot he chose, then parked immediately next to the elevator door, in a tiny spot reserved for bicycles.

As Joseph walked up to the elevator door, he raised his eyebrows at Eric's choice of parking spots.

Eric shrugged. "I'll pay the ticket."

They got into the elevator and Joseph punched the button for the fifteenth floor. They rode in silence for a few moments. Finally Joseph spoke. "I want one thing clear. You said that if it turns out that this is an elaborate stunt on your part to try to get my daughter back, that I won't ever have to see you again. I want your word that you won't ever chase after her again."

Eric raised his eyebrows. "Chase after *her*? I've never chased after Mel."

Joseph was the one to raise his eyebrows now. When he spoke, the words were dripping with sarcasm. "Oh really? She says she's seen you many times since high school. How exactly was that possible, unless you drove out to her college to pester her, while she was supposed to be studying?"

Eric spoke quietly, looking Joseph directly in the eye. "She drove out to see me, sir."

"What?"

Eric nodded, continuing to look directly into the older

man's eyes. "She used to drive out sometimes without telling you that she was in town. She did that for years. But I honestly haven't seen her in about three years, since she graduated and got her veterinary practice going. The last time she came to see me I told her to go away—that I was tired of being her *dirty little secret* that she kept hidden from everyone in her life."

Eric cleared his throat. "When she showed up at my family's cabin in Michigan, it was because she remembered how to get there from having been there years ago. I swear I had no idea she was going there."

Joseph was having trouble processing what the younger man had said, but he was spared from having to respond when the door opened on the fifteenth floor. Joseph strode purposefully down the hall with Eric trailing right behind him. He stopped before one of the doors and knocked loudly. There wasn't any response. Joseph leaned over and rang the doorbell, then knocked again.

Eric reached over to push the doorbell in—and held it in.

They heard a voice from inside, then the door was unlocked and thrown open.

"Yeah, yeah, what the hell do you want?" Donald was wearing boxer shorts and a tee shirt. He was unshaven with tousled hair, and barefoot. His jaw dropped open in shock when he saw who was standing at his door.

Joseph nodded at him briefly. "Hello Donald. I want to talk to my daughter."

Joseph pushed past Donald who was trying unsuccessfully, to block the door. Eric followed the older man in and began to look around.

"This is a surprise, Joseph." Donald appeared very nervous.

Joseph addressed him sternly. "Where is my daughter? Tell her I want to speak to her immediately."

Donald tried to change the subject by staring at Eric. "And just who the hell are you? No wait—don't tell me. Grease on your hands, a leather jacket. You must be the biker boyfriend from high school that Maribel told me about."

Joseph's eyebrows shot up. "*Maribel* called you and told you about him?"

Donald was glaring at Eric. "Yeah. She wanted me to know that some asshole from way back in Pamela's past was trying to ruin her life again. She asked me to help her make sure that Pamela didn't make a huge mistake. But no worries about that anymore."

"Oh? Why?" Eric spoke through gritted teeth.

"We're getting married as soon as I can book us a flight to Vegas."

Eric pursed his lips, then inclined his head towards the hallway. "Then you won't mind if I search the rooms, just to make sure that Mel isn't in any kind of trouble?"

Donald started, shaking his head. "She's—uh—she's not here. She's out shopping. Women—you know. Got to have new clothes for every little occasion. Like an elopement."

Joseph spoke very quietly, in a voice that his fellow attorneys had learned a long time ago to fear. "So my daughter is not here now, is that what you are saying?"

Donald nodded. "Yeah, she's sh—" He watched as Eric took his cell phone out of his jacket pocket. "Hey, what are you doing?"

Eric gave him a tight smile. "Calling Mel's number."

Donald tried to grab for the phone, but it was too late. The sound of the ringing could be heard coming from one of the rooms down the hall.

Eric took off quickly in the direction of the sound, with Joseph right behind him. Donald tried to cut them both off at the door, but Eric was too quick for him, and Joseph pushed him out of the way.

Eric threw open the door to see Pamela lying naked on the floor, curled into a fetal position, her phone still in her hand.

Joseph had felt before that moment, as if all the shocks in his life were behind him. That life was good and easy now, and nothing could ever hurt him again. He'd been wrong.

Donald started to sputter. "What the hell are you doing, Pamela? I thought you were going shopping."

Eric ran to her side and shook her shoulder gently, saying her name softly but distinctly. "Mel. Mel, honey, it's me. Eric. I'm here."

Pamela's eyelids fluttered, as if she were trying to open her eyes, but they weren't cooperating.

Eric knelt beside her and lifted the top half of her into his lap. He cradled her shoulders, while her head lolled backwards, then rolled from side to side.

With great effort, she opened her eyes.

Eric's face was inches from hers.

Her lips curled up in a grimace as she tried to smile. "Eric! I knew you would come. Tha's why I called you—" Her head lolled back again.

Donald looked over to see Joseph talking into his cell phone. "What are you doing?"

Joseph's face alone should have been enough to frighten him. "Calling the police, and an ambulance."

"You can't do that!"

"Just watch me."

Donald started to sidle out of the room.

Joseph quickly moved to take up all the space of the doorway. "You'll have to go through me to get out of here, boy."

"You have to let me make a phone call," Donald whined.

Joseph shook his head. "Not yet I don't. You can make that call from the station. That's when you'll need a lawyer. I'll have your ass thrown in jail for this."

After a short, uncomfortable wait, the EMTs arrived

accompanied by two police officers, and the room was crowded with people.

Eric had grabbed a sheet off the bed and wrapped Pamela partially in it, so that she was not totally nude.

One of the police officers began to ask questions. "Who's the one who made the call?"

Joseph stepped forward. "That would be me, officer. My name is Joseph Wilson. I'm her father." He nodded towards Pamela.

She was being laid onto a stretcher, with Eric still holding her hand.

The female EMT shot out her questions. "Who gave her the drugs? And what kind was it?"

Joseph inclined his head towards Donald, who was trying to appear as inconspicuous as possible. "He did. Ask him."

The police officers surrounded Donald, cutting off any possibility of his getting out of the door.

He started to talk, cleared his throat, and began again. "Uh, rohypnol. You know — roofies."

Joseph exploded. "You son of a bitch! You gave my daughter the date-rate drug?"

Eric stood up and surged forward, aiming at Donald's throat.

Joseph was close to him and had a shot of adrenalin in his system that made him quicker and strong enough to hold the younger man back.

Meanwhile the female EMT kept getting information. "How much and when?"

Donald shrugged casually. "I dunno. Some in her bottle of champagne yesterday. A little bit more this morning in her water. She — uh — said she needed calming down a bit. After all of her recent excitement."

"And this fresh bruising around her buttocks?" The EMT had lifted the sheet a little and was expertly checking Pamela.

"And on her thighs?" She stared at Donald, her expression hardening.

"She—I—we're living together. She likes it rough. Some women are like that."

"So you fed her rohypnol and then when she was like this—almost unconscious—you engaged in rough sex?" The EMT stared at Donald, then Joseph, and finally nodded at one of the cops. Without another word she motioned at her assistant and continued getting Pamela ready to move.

Eric struggled with Joseph for just a minute. He stopped and looked intently into the older man's eyes and spoke quietly. "Just let me at him, sir. I'll be quick. I just need to hurt him."

Joseph shook his head. "No. *I'll* hurt him."

The police were busy taking down information from a sullen Donald. The EMTs were getting ready to move Pamela.

Eric struggled again briefly.

Joseph held onto him and spoke urgently to him in a low voice. "Listen to me, son. He's from my world. I know how to hurt him much better than you do. You hit him, he'll heal. Then he'll sue you for assault and battery. But with what I'm going to hit him with, he'll never recover."

Eric looked into his eyes. "I'm listening."

"I know the owners of his firm. I golf with them. Believe me, he's going to spend the rest of his life regretting this."

Donald glared at them as one police officer put handcuffs on him and led him out of the apartment. The other officer approached Joseph. "You need to come down to the station in order to press charges."

Joseph nodded.

Eric moved over to grab for Pamela's hand again.

The EMTs tried to stop him. "Hey, you can't touch her. We're taking her down to the hospital."

"Can I ride with her?"

The female EMT looked him in the eye. "Are you related to her?"

Eric shook his head.

Joseph cleared his throat before he spoke. "He's her fiancé. Please allow him to accompany her in the ambulance."

Eric gave him a quick grateful look, which Joseph returned with a curt nod. He then turned and followed the second officer out of the apartment.

Eric situated himself in the ambulance right next to Pamela's head. She never opened her eyes, but he kept holding onto her hand all during the ride. He spoke softly to her. "Hold on, babe. Please, Mel. Hold on. I won't leave your side."

The ambulance ride seemed to take forever.

Chapter Sixteen

Three hours later Joseph Wilson walked into the room that his daughter was lying in, to find that Eric was still by her side. He was holding her hand and talking quietly to her. She wasn't speaking but watching his face intently. Eric looked up when he walked in.

Joseph's steps were slow, as if the weight of the world were on his shoulders. He felt as if the past few hours were a surreal nightmare, yet because it was real, he felt as if he had aged a hundred years in just a few hours. "I called Maribel. She's on her way. She was at the spa and has to have them take all of the stuff off her, so she can get dressed to meet us here."

Eric nodded, turning back to watch Pamela.

Joseph walked over to the other side of the bed and smoothed a lock of hair back from her face. He looked around and pulled another chair over from the wall and sat on the opposite side of the bed from Eric. They sat silently in vigil for a few moments.

When Joseph broke the silence his words sounded painfully spoken. "There's one thing that's still bothering me, Pamela. I'm your father. Why didn't you call *me*? Why did you call *him* instead of me?"

Eric looked down at the bed and Pamela nodded, letting him speak for her.

He turned to Joseph and shrugged. "I asked her about that. She said she was afraid you wouldn't have believed her. Like you didn't want to believe me."

That was the answer that Joseph had feared. For a moment

he lost control over himself. He put his face down into his hands, his shoulders shaking with overwhelming anguish.

Eric had had enough experience with grief in his life, to know that his only place was to bear silent witness. The room was quiet and still, with the only noises the comings and goings of people in the hallway.

Pamela struggled to lift her hand, reaching over to pat her father's head awkwardly.

Suddenly a loud, shrill voice could be heard coming closer to them.

"Where is she? Where is my daughter?"

Joseph looked up quickly and his eyes met Eric's with an unspoken supplication. Eric nodded slightly, and an understanding passed between them. The two men who loved Pamela the most in the world, looked up as her mother pushed into the room, a force of nature not to be denied.

"Pamela!" She ran over to the bed, obviously planning on hurling herself onto the still form of her daughter.

Joseph grabbed his wife as she tried to push past him, and he held her still. "No, Maribel. Just sit quietly for a minute."

"Why can't I talk to her?"

"You can—just don't make a big production out of it. I spoke to the doctor. They pumped her stomach. She's on an IV of fluids because that drug really dehydrates you."

She turned to glare at Eric. "Why is *he* here?"

Joseph never got a chance to answer her.

Pamela chose that moment to clear her throat and speak, though it looked painful. "Eric's here because I asked him to help me, Mom. You should be grateful that he did. I am."

Eric leaned over to place a chaste kiss on her cheek. "I love you, Mel. I had to come."

She smiled back at him with love shining in her eyes.

That was more than her mother could stand. "Pamela! What is all of this about?"

Pamela turned to her mother and frowned. "Didn't they tell you what happened? What Donald was doing to me?"

Maribel looked shocked and horrified. She nodded. "Yes, but of course, I don't believe any of it. Donald wouldn't do such a thing to you. He loves you."

Pamela shook her head. "No, Mom. He drugged me and raped me—repeatedly. I don't remember much of anything. But he'd tell me before I passed out what he was planning on doing to me next." She shuddered.

Eric gripped her hand harder.

Maribel sputtered, still trying to force her world to make sense. "But when I called your number this morning, he said you were sleeping. He said you were planning on eloping. He said—" She stopped and looked beseechingly at her husband, who shook his head.

"No, Maribel. He had drugged her and was keeping her naked in the bedroom. She was so drugged that she barely made it to the desk where her cell phone was. And we're all lucky that she did. And I'm glad that she—" His voice broke in a sound suspiciously like a sob. He swallowed and cleared his throat, before he continued. "I'm glad that she thought to call Eric. He moved heaven and earth to get to her. We owe him everything."

Maribel shook her head. "But what about Donald?"

Joseph's face changed to stone. He spoke tonelessly. "He's in a jail cell as we speak. He'll be out soon enough, but he'll be seeing me in the very near future. He's going to want to make a deal to save his ass. But he's not going to like my terms, I can promise you that."

The nurse bustled into the room to find her patient awake and responsive. She shooed them all out of way while she took Pamela's vital signs, then she turned to smile at all of them. "The doctor will be around to check on her soon. He's probably going to want her to stay the night, just to be sure that she's fully recovered."

"And of course you will be coming home for a few days, Pamela, so that I can take care of you." While she spoke, Maribel glared over the bed at Eric.

He met her gaze blandly, surprising them all by smiling at her and nodding.

Pamela protested. "But Mom, I want to move—"

Eric touched her face and she turned to look at him. "Mel, it's probably a better idea for you to spend a couple of days having your mom spoil you. I already had to take today off work. I can't take another couple of days off. But I only work a half-day on Saturday."

"Will you come to see me every night after work?"

Maribel let out a breath that sounded suspiciously like a hiss.

Joseph cleared his throat and tightened his arm around her shoulders.

Eric smiled at Pamela. "If you want me to."

Pamela nodded and smiled. "And will you help me move my stuff into your place over the weekend?"

There was silence from her parents.

Eric looked up at them, met their gaze, then looked back down at the woman he had always loved.

"Yes, babe. I'll rent a truck so we can do it in one trip. How's that?"

Pamela nodded. "Good."

Maribel found her voice. "Pamela, are you sure? This is so sudden."

Pamela grinned weakly. "Sudden? Mom, I've been in love with him for twelve years. I don't call that sudden."

"But don't you think you need some time to think things over? I mean after all that has happened?"

Joseph cleared his throat. "Maribel, I think we should leave them alone to talk. Why don't you and I go grab some dinner on the way home? It's been too many hours since I ate any-thing. My stomach is burning from hunger. And stress."

"But Joseph—"

The look in his eyes was enough to make her decide that his suggestion was a good one. First she bent over and kissed her daughter on the cheek. "I was so worried about you, Pamela."

Pamela smiled weakly. "You don't have to worry about me anymore, Mom. Eric will take good care of me."

Maribel raised her manicured eyebrows at him.

Eric nodded solemnly at her.

Joseph spoke. "I'm sure he will honey. He's already proven that today. Let's go, Maribel."

At the door, he turned to see Eric leaning over to kiss Pamela, and he smiled.

Chapter Seventeen

Late on Thursday afternoon, Joseph waited in his office for his next appointment. He looked up when there was a knock. The door opened to reveal Donald, all cleaned up and in a suit and tie, along with his attorney.

Joseph frowned at them both. "I said I wanted to speak to you alone, Donald."

Both men started to object.

Joseph sighed heavily. "All right. If you really want to take this all the way to a jury trial, I guess that's the way we'll play it then."

The attorney shot a quick glance at Joseph before leaning closer to speak directly into Donald's ear. He then turned and walked out the room.

Donald reluctantly walked over to the chair in front of the massive desk that Joseph sat behind.

"So what do you want? What's your terms?" Donald didn't bother to hide his animosity or his sullen temper.

Joseph began to tap his pencil on the desk in front of him as he considered his words carefully. "I guess spending time in jail didn't do much to improve your manners. Well, boy, there's a few ways we can play this out. One is I take you all the way to court and drag your name through the mud. Of course, that will result in you losing not only any chance you ever had to make partner, but you will lose your job as well. And there won't be a firm in the city who will take a chance on hiring a lawyer who has been convicted of drugging and raping a woman. I'd love to see the odds that bookies will give, of you living through your jail sentence. Not only will you be the fresh new meat, with blond hair and a baby face, but I understand you have some enemies in there, and they have long memories."

Donald's face blanched as he swallowed hard.

"Of course, I must admit I'm really partial to the idea of you finding out what it feels like to be drugged and raped. But I'm trying to keep my vindictive nature under control."

Donald swallowed hard again.

Joseph continued tapping the pencil as he spoke. "Another way we can do this, is I drop all charges and you walk free."

Donald leaned forward expectantly.

Joseph shook his head. "But that's not going to happen, boy. You drugged and raped my daughter. The only thing that's stopping me from killing you myself, is that my life has been dedicated to upholding the laws of our land. I'm not about to let an insignificant piece of shit like you take me down with you."

He leaned forward. "So now we come to what's *really* going to happen. I spoke with your senior partners yesterday. They know all about what you did. Making partner is out of the question—at least for the next few decades. Probably forever. They're going to make sure that you get the crappiest cases, and more work than you can handle. If you want to stay with them, you are going to have to keep your nose to the grindstone and prove yourself to them every day, as if you just started there.

Donald found his voice but stuttered. "Th-th-they're—n-not f-f-firing me?"

Joseph shook his head. "No. I have agreed to drop all charges."

Donald smiled in relief.

Joseph shook his head more emphatically. "But don't think for one minute that I'm doing this for you. I'm only thinking of my daughter. I'm dropping the charges because Pamela doesn't deserve to have to sit in court and hear you testify all about exactly how you raped her and how many times. She's getting her life back together again, and she's getting married — to the *right* man this time. You're not going to be a part of her life ever again."

Donald started to relax.

Joseph got up and walked slowly over to stand directly in front of Donald. He took a deep breath then grabbed the arms of the chair and picked it up, with Donald still sitting in it, and lifted it up into the air to hold Donald at his eye level. "But you listen to me, boy, and you listen good. I may have left the ghetto behind when I went away to college, but the ghetto is still in me. I can call in a few favors to *get things done*. You are to stay away from my daughter, from her man Eric, and from any family they may ever have. You are *not* to contact any of them in any way, shape or form. If I ever even *suspect* that you have so much as sneezed in her direction, it will be the last thing that you ever do. I will make a call. It will be as painful for you as I can arrange. And fatal — eventually."

He abruptly dropped the chair.

Donald's head snapped back as the chair hit the floor with a loud thud.

"Do I make myself clear, boy?"

Donald nodded vigorously. "Yes, sir."

"Good. Now get out of my sight. You sicken me. I don't ever want to have to look at you again. Understand?"

Donald jumped up from the chair, still nodding. He walked quickly over to the door, opened it, and fell through it, in his eagerness to be out of the room.

Joseph sat back with a long sigh, shaking his head, his heart still racing from the burst of adrenaline he had channeled to be able to make a show of superior strength. Now he just felt old and weary and spoke to the thin air.

"I still wish I could have just killed you myself. But this will be more painful for you in the long run. And this way I'll know where you're at and what you're doing. I'll have to be content with that."

Then he called Pamela to let her know that this painful episode in her life was over.

CHAPTER EIGHTEEN

Two months later, Pamela and Eric strolled slowly back to their apartment. They had just had dinner with her parents, who had told them that their wedding gift to them was going to be the down payment on a house of their choosing.

Eric shook his head. "Why are they doing that? They don't even like me."

"Maybe it's because you made such a good impression on my dad—this time. Mom's still not fond of you, but she's trying to accept the inevitable."

"I used to think that your dad didn't like me, either."

She smiled at him. "When we were in high school, he didn't. But then you know how dads are. He was probably convinced that you were only after one thing, with his baby girl!"

"That's not true at all," he answered heatedly. "I was after two things—your great tits, and your hot pussy." He grinned.

She shrugged off his arm that had been resting on her shoulders. She punched at it.

"Oh, and let's not forget your mouth too. You got really good with that, after some practice. And there's your fine ass. So I guess it was four things I was after."

"Eric Taylor, sometimes you are such a pig. I really don't know what I see in you" She stomped ahead of him, yelling back at him over her shoulder.

He quickly caught up with her, grabbed her, and pulled her roughly to him, to kiss her in a frenzy of passion, ignoring any looks they might have drawn from curious pedestrians who had to circle around them to pass. "You belong to me, remember?" He muttered into her ear, his lips trailing a pathway down her face, his hot breath blowing on her skin, sending chills down her spine, as her toes curled visibly, in her sandals.

"Yes." She twined her arms up and around him, under his shirt, rubbing at his back muscles. She ground her pelvis against him. "Race you back home?"

"You expect me to be able to run like this?" He shoved his pelvis forward, to show her what her attentions had done to him.

"No. That's why I challenged you. You'll have to pole-vault home, and I'm going to beat your ass in the door. That means that I get to be on top this time. Last one home gets the bottom."

She took off, running remarkably well for someone in high-heeled sandals. She did beat him back to their apartment building lobby, but only just barely. They both panted, waiting for the elevator.

Eric was the one to catch his breath first. "I just let you win, you know. I don't care who's on top, as long as we get to have wild monkey sex all night!"

She patted the side of his face, rubbing her palm along the stubble that never seemed to go away. "And now that I'm not on the pill anymore, we need to keep on practicing until we get really good at it. Then maybe it will catch, and we'll get pregnant."

"Let's get started on practicing right now." He pulled her close again, and kissed her long and hard, groping all his favorite places. When the elevator bell rang, he danced her into it, hit the button for their floor over her shoulder, then leaned back against the wall, holding her close and groping her as they rode up to their floor.

And she did get to be on top the first time. After that, they took turns, and both were totally fine with that until they fell asleep from satisfied exhaustion.

Chapter Nineteen

As she decorated the bedroom with yet another lit candle, Pamela took a quick glance around the room, to be sure every detail was right. She smiled as she glanced at the embroidered cross-stitch over the bed, a wedding gift from Diane, that said, *Happiness is Being Married to Your Best Friend.*

The satin sheets were on the bed, and the covers were turned down. The windows were open just enough to let a cool breeze in, but the blinds were closed so none of the neighbors would be able to watch just what it was that they did, that made her scream and yell so much.

Hearing Eric coming in the door, she made sure that her negligee was adjusted to give her maximum cleavage, and she turned to welcome her man into the room.

"They're both finally asleep," he sighed "I put Joey back into the crib. Jonathan promised to come get us if his brother wakes him up again. Let's hope they give us more time than the last time." He grinned at her.

"Hey, Jonathan will be at his mom's next weekend, right? Besides, we have right now, and that's all that matters." She moved closer to hug him, enjoying the feel of the silk robe that she had given to him. "Besides, if we are going to keep on with this baby-making thing, we're going to have to learn to take our pleasure whenever we can, right?"

He used a hand to twirl one of her curls. He wound his hands into her hair, tilted her face upwards, and lowered his head to kiss her, long, lovingly, and hard. "Not so different from when we were young, and had to look for places to screw, keeping one eye out for the cops and the other on the time."

She sighed at their happy shared memories. "Who knew we'd end up here, back then?"

"*I* did." His lips were busy kissing her neck, his hands massaging her back, down to her buttocks, and back up again.

"You did?" She took his hand and led him over to their bed. She lay back on it, pulling at the belt that held his robe closed.

He tossed the robe onto the floor, and she held out her arms. He moved into them and sighed with pleasure. "Yes." He moved her spaghetti straps aside, to lick and kiss at her neck and shoulders, his hands busy rubbing at her through the silk.

"Oooh, keep on doing that, Mr. Taylor! And happy anniversary, my love."

He smiled at her as he pulled her negligee off, and drank in the sight of his woman, arching her back and signaling welcome to any touch he might want to do. "After all, from that first night, you have been *she-who-belongs-to-Eric*. Marrying you and making you Mrs. Taylor, was just a formality."

She moaned in satisfaction, as his lips trailed a path from her breast, to her neck, then up to her lips.

"I'm so glad that I finally made the right choice in my life."

"Me too." He surged forward to lay claim to her body once again—something that neither of them ever got tired of.

As they moved together, he panted out his words of love. "I'm glad that you weren't a runaway bride at *our* wedding. And I get to spend the rest of my life expressing what I have always felt for you—my only love."

She sighed with happiness. "And we make such beautiful kids."

His lips claimed hers and his tongue urgently probed her mouth. "Let's make another one." He pushed his hips forward and felt her start to spasm out of control.

Her only answer was to moan in pleasure.

He chuckled softly. "I'll take that as a *yes*."

About the Author

Mom taught me to read when I was five. Since then, I have always had characters intruding into my thoughts, showing scenes from their lives. When I ignore them, they start to yell louder. If I write their stories so they can live in readers' heads as well, they usually leave me alone . . .until the next voices appear. I like the noise.

Learn more about me and my books, read excerpts and reviews, at: www.fionamcgier.com

Or come visit me on Facebook: https://www.facebook.com/fiona.mcgier/